What Kind Of Love Is This?

3

Captivating A Boss

Tina J

Copyright 2018

More Books by Tina J

Lamar

"Grandma, my dad doesn't want me around uncle Lamar." I heard my niece say over the phone. My mom called to see her since it's been a while. She had her on speaker because I wanted to know why we hadn't seen her either.

"What do you mean Raina? He's your uncle and I'm your grandmother. Your mom would not approve of what he's doing?"

"Grandma, the woman who molested me, caught me at uncle Lamar's house. He was supposed to protect me from her but he wanted to be nasty with his dirty girlfriend and left me to fend for myself. She did bad things to me in that house." I felt like shit listening to her say that and my mom gave me the evilest look ever. She knew about the bitch Veronica bullying and touching my niece but she had no idea, I let the shit happen in my house. Thinking with my dick, allowed my niece to be violated and I was fucked up over it. I only found out because

4

this is the hundredth time my mom tried to see Raina and she wasn't tryna come around me.

"I understand Raina but my house isn't the same."

"I know but he may pop up and I don't wanna see him."

"But your dad let it happen."

"NO HE DIDN'T. HE HAD NO IDEA WHAT SHE WAS DOING AND WHEN HE DID, SHE COULDN'T BE AROUND ME ANYMORE. AND STOP BRINGING UP MY MOM WOULD HAVE A FIT AND THAT MY DAD LET IT HAPPEN." Raina snapped and my mom was pissed.

"Little girl, don't talk to me like that. I am still the adult and…"

"Then act like it grandma and understand where I'm coming from. I'm not saying uncle Lamar would hurt me but you're tryna put me in a position to be around someone, I don't wanna be. Why can't you understand?" You could hear Raina crying and some noise in the background. Someone was asking her, if she were ok.

"Hello. Is anyone there?" The woman spoke and I had no idea who she was.

"Yea, why is my niece pretending like she doesn't wanna be around us? What y'all over there poisoning her with lies?" I was fed up at this point.

"I'll be right back Raina."

"But I don't wanna go over there." I heard my niece whining in the background. My mom asked who the woman was and I had no idea. It could be the chick Khloe, Risky was dealing with but then again, I heard he was with the therapist or some shit.

"And you're not. Give me a minute." You could hear a door close and the woman got back on the phone.

"Hi, who am I speaking to?"

"This is her uncle Lamar."

"Hi Lamar, this is Khloe, Ryan's fiancé." *His fiancé?* This nigga didn't even ask to marry my sister and he's about to tie the know with some fat bitch. Hell yea, I had a problem with it.

"Raina doesn't want to come over there but your mom is more than welcome to meet us somewhere or…" I cut her fat ass right off.

"Now you listen to me bitch."

"Bitch?"

"You heard me. My mom has her own house and don't need to meet her grandmother anywhere, but here. Second, who the fuck you think you are tryna dictate shit? I'm her uncle and if I wanna see her, then bring her the fuck over. Do I make myself clear?" I didn't hear anything.

"Hello?"

"I'm here. I was waiting for you to finish. Can I speak now?"

"Go the fuck head."

"First off motherfucker, don't ever think its ok to disrespect me, your niece or your sister."

"My sister? What the fuck you talking about?"

"The minute you allowed the stupid bitch to attack and violate your niece in yo pissy ass house, you disrespected her. All so you can get your little dick sucked by some dirty bitch.

7

Then you wanna call Raina all types of spoiled brats and a whiny bitch because she doesn't wanna be around you."

"What?"

"Oh, I've seen the nasty text messages you sent her because she doesn't wanna be around you. You and I both know, if her father saw these you wouldn't even be on this phone bitching like a chick. Last but not least, don't call this phone again telling her she better come see you or your mother because it ain't happening, captain."

"Bitch, you're not her mother."

"You're right but I'm gonna be her stepmother and no one is gonna bully, torture or make my daughter feel obligated to see them if she doesn't want to. You of all people should respect it after everything she's been through but you're so fucking selfish and tryna bully her into coming there. What would your sister say to you allowing her daughter to be attacked while she was in your care? Huh? How would she feel knowing you fucked the very same woman who did it? Or the fact you're tryna kill Raina's father over jealousy?" How the fuck did she know all that?

8

"Exactly! Stay silent motherfucker and don't dial this number again because if you do, I can promise you that Ryan, Waleed or even myself will put a fucking bullet in between your eyes now fuck with it, if you want." I looked down at the phone and noticed she hung up. I tried to call back but the number was blocked.

"What the hell is wrong with you Lamar? Did you sleep with the woman who dud those things to Raina? Are you trying to kill her father?"

"Ma, you don't understand."

"Jesus, please be a fence. My son is going to be buried right next to his sister." She stood up.

"Really!"

"Yes because you're going after a dangerous man. He will do anything for Raina and if that woman is indeed his fiancé, he will go to war for her. You know that because he was the same with your sister. Lamar, leave the state or something. Please, I can't lose another child." I stood there in shock listening to my own mother wish death on me and tell me to leave the state in the same breath. Why wasn't anyone

9

listening to me about Risky being the one who got her killed? Do I have to spell it out? Matter of fact, I'm gonna do one better and make that nigga wish he never knew me or my sister.

****

Its been a little over a week since the Khloe bitch talked all that bullshit and hung up on me but I was still mad. Who the hell did she think she was, tryna tell me right from wrong? If my memory serves me correctly that punk nigga, still fucked Veronica after she made her throw up too. She had some nerve tryna call me out when her damn man ain't shit. I know that because I'm sitting outside the doctor's office snapping pictures of him hugging some other bitch. Nigga got a whole fiancé at home and he still fishing.

"Hello." I answered the call from the dude who was about to be my new boss and allow me to run shit.

"Meet me at the address I'm sending to your phone in fifteen minutes."

"Got it." I snapped a few more photos and the best one was of the chick placing her lips on his. I couldn't wait to show the stuck-up bitch, this one.

I drove to the spot he told me to meet him at, which was a damn strip mall. There weren't a lotta people there but it wouldn't be since damn near everything was closed, except the pharmacy. I was about to send him a text asking where he was when this chick stepped out this nice ass truck. I waited to see what she would do and once she went in the pharmacy, I followed. You could hear her asking for some Robotusssin and a few other over the counter medicines. One of them must be sick and right now I don't care who because she and I, are about to have some fun. She grabbed the bag from the lady and walked out the door, with my creepy ass right behind her.

"What up bitch? Talk that shit now." She turned around with no facial expression.

"Well, well, well. We meet again, I see." I was shocked she remembered me.

"You damn right, now you're gonna take a ride with me."

"The hell I am. My man is at home waiting for me and."

"Actual facts you're lying." She folded her arms across her chest.

"Oh yea. How the fuck you know?"

"Because I just left him with his other bitch." I pulled my phone out and showed her all the photos of her nigga hugged up.

"Yea, look at the time and date. Ain't no need to lie. Yo nigga is as grimy as the rest of us." I could see how watery her eyes got.

"Get in the car." I pointed to my ride.

"No." She moved past me.

"GET IN THE FUCKING CAR!" I shouted and put my gun on the side of her waist. She walked over to it and I heard someone call my name. I couldn't make out the voice.

"Hello, Khloe." Her eyes got real big.

"I think the three of us should take a ride. What you think Lamar?" He said and I didn't say a word. I made my way to the black suburban waiting on the other side of the parking

lot. Who is this nigga and what type of shit Khloe got going n?

Julie

"Yo, you pregnant yet?" Oscar asked and picked the test up. I took tissue off the roll and wiped myself.

"You tell me since the test is in your hand."

WHAP! My face turned sideways from the force his hand caused.

"What I tell you about talking shit?" I wiped the blood off my lip.

"And you promised my sister would be dead by now but we can't always get what we want."

Hell yea, I'm sleeping with the exact nigga who's supposed to marry my sister. A man like Oscar needs a ride or die, beautiful and loyal chick by his side. Luna is nothing of the sort. She's fat, thinks her shit don't stink and after putting me in the hospital some years ago, I'm gonna make sure to return the favor. The only difference is her hospital visit will be to the morgue.

I'm sure her fat ass told the story of how we're related but let me reiterate it a little. Evidently, my mom was a ho and sleeping with a taken man. I say evidently because she was dead before I was old enough to ask questions. Anyway, she popped up pregnant, had the baby and supposedly tried to use me as a pawn in getting him back.

Luna's mom found out and left him. He was devastated and spent tons of money, countless hours of tryna make it up and even terminated my mom, in order to get her to come home. His wife, my stepmom sat me down and explained it to me one day but I still blamed her. Had she not left him, my mother would still be here. She tried to tell me my mom made many attempts on her life but I didn't believe it. Like I said, I was too young to know anything and since she's not here to defend herself, I can think what I want.

Now the way Oscar and I met is because after leaving the ICU unit Luna put me in, I ran off to Mexico to hide. I was scared my father would find and kill me. For the first two years, I got a job and since the pay is so low, I had to stay in homeless shelters because I couldn't afford anywhere to live. I

15

met some chick in the store who took pity on me and introduced me to the stripping life.

Fortunately for me, Oscar owned it. The first day we met, he asked if I were a virgin because the men there, may or may not want sex. Once I told him yes, he never allowed me to strip. I had to be a bottle girl and ended up his woman.

We have two kids together but they came a couple of years ago. We had to keep them a secret because of the stupid ass agreement between him and my sister.

If you're wondering how I was able to be with Waleed, it's because I caught Oscar cheating and left him. I moved back to Jersey because I figured enough time passed and my father wouldn't be looking for me. I met Waleed at a club up north and the two of us hooked up. I figured Oscar was doing his thing so why not do me?

Waleed and I stayed together for a while, I got pregnant and terminated it. Oscar said, I'd never have kids with another man and begged me to come home, which is why I left. But not before sleeping with Lamar to piss him off. Waleed can say he didn't cheat all he wants but a woman knows when her man steps out. I didn't care how hurt he was because my real man wanted me home and I went running.

Now we're sitting here waiting on the results of a pregnancy test. I grabbed his hand and glanced at the test. When I looked up he was smiling.

"Now let's go put our plan in motion. I'm tired of waiting." He stepped out and I followed.

"Oscar?" He turned to look at me.

"Damn, you sexy. Can I get some before we go?" I asked.

"I don't know, can you?" He smirked and pulled the back of my hair and had me staring in his face.

"You do know it's gonna be a war?"

"I do."

"Who you riding for?"

"My man. What you think this is?" The two of us fucked the hell outta one another and got ready to get rid of my sister and allow him to take his seat on the throne.

****

"When she comes out Julie don't get stupid." Oscar said as we waited for Luna to emerge from the mall. It was Saturday and packed like crazy, which made it even better because no one would be paying us any mind.

"I got it Oscar. I'm not an amateur."

"Not in bed, that's for sure." I turned and kissed his lips.

"She's on her way out boss." One of the guys spoke in the walkie talkie.

"Its time."

I hopped out the car and hurried to the door, she supposedly was coming out of and ran straight into her. She pushed the shit outta me and two big ass men came outta nowhere. We were prepared for her bodyguards so when their bodies hit the ground, Luna appeared to be afraid and that's exactly the way I wanted it. People were running and yelling but no one stopped to ask if either of us needed help.

"What the fuck you want Julie?" I saw her text on the phone and then place it in her back pocket. Not knowing if it was Waleed or not I had to hurry up. She started speed walking

18

in the parking lot, which pissed me off because I had heels on. I pulled her arm and she stopped.

"I just wanna know if you're gonna be a good stepmother to my child?"

"WHAT?"

"Yea bitch. Me and Waleed are expecting."

"What up Luna?" Oscar said and it looked like all the blood drained from her face. I mean, she was scared to death for some reason.

"Oscar, whattt… what… are you doing here?"

"I came to shop but who knew I'd run into you? Are you ok? You look pale."

"Ummm. No, I'm fine." She was still stuttering. And once she tried to move past, the bags in front of her fell and I now knew why she was scared.

CLICK! Oscar had his gun out.

"You better tell me you're fucking bloated because by the size of your stomach, I'd say you were pregnant." He snatched her by the hair, placed the gun under her chin and asked again.

"Oscar please." She had tears racing down her face.

"Did you get married?" I asked lifting her hand up, after seeing that huge ass rock on her finger. Oscar's entire demeanor changed and I swore the devil himself came out.

"Bitch! Are you married?" He asked and in a matter of five seconds everything went from sugar to shit.

Khloe

"Are you ok?" Mr. Suarez, who is Luna's father asked as we moved towards the truck. When he showed up I was surprised because he's never on this side of town.

I ran over here to the pharmacy to grab the medicine for Raina. She had the flu shot the other day and wasn't feeling well. The doctor said most likely she got it and it had to run through her body. He did put her on a few antibiotics because of the ear infection, she also had.

He told me I could get some over the counter cough medicine if I wanted but the medicine would kick right in. Raina, swore she was dying and you couldn't tell her different. I mean she asked me to take her temperature like five times. Then she needed soup, crackers and a bunch of other shit. Ryan told me she was getting on his nerves so he was going out. Men never could handle kids when they're sick.

Then I get here and dumb ass Lamar, couldn't wait to show me photos of Ryan and some woman. It appeared to be the Sandy chick but to be honest, the guys back was too the side and he resembled my man but I'm not so sure it's him. I wanna ask him about it but he and I are in a good space right now and I don't wanna make accusations and they're false. A lot of relationships fail when you start believing outsiders, then your own man.

"I'm fine. This is the second time Lamar has tried to attack me."

"The second time?" He questioned. I filled him in on when we originally met and how I had to mace his ugly ass.

"You obviously have an issue with women but it's nothing we can't fix." Mr. S, hit Lamar so hard, he stumbled back and almost fell. One of his bodyguards caught him and I didn't understand why, at first. Shit, he could've fallen and cracked his head open for all I care.

The bodyguard tied him up and tossed Lamar in the trunk. You could hear him rolling around and yelling. It was actually funny listening to him yell out like a girl. Who knew a big, black ugly dude like him would be scared? I guess that's why he always fucked with women and not men. Mr. S, held the door open for me to get in. I had my car here and could've

drive myself but I wouldn't dare disobey him. Not that he'd

hurt me but I had too much respect for him to go against what

he says.

"Wait! I have to take this medication to Raina." He

nodded and told me to hand it over to his bodyguard. I told him

she's at the house with her grandmother. Even though

Veronica is gone, I was still nervous about leaving her alone

and so was Ryan. She tried to tell us it's ok but neither of us

were tryna hear it.

"How do you know Lamar?" I asked when we got in

his truck.

"Khloe there's a war about to start with the man Luna

was supposed to marry, and the man she did marry." I sucked

my teeth and turned my head. Did he really ask me to come

along to speak about his daughter? If so, he could've left me

right where I was.

"I understand you're mad because she's like your sister

and you have every right to be. But Ima need you to grow the

fuck up and get over it." I snapped my neck.

23

"I don't give a fuck if you're not in the other wedding Luna wants to have, or the godmother to my grandson. My concern is you pretending not to have hid things from her."

"Excuse me!" I folded my arms across my chest.

"Let me ask you this." He turned to look at me.

"Yoooo get me the fuck outta here." You heard Lamar yell. Mr. S, punched him in the face and he was knocked out.

"Now. Back to what I was saying." He stretched his hand in and out after punching Lamar. There was a small scratch on it but other than that, nothing. Mr. S, isn't a man you wanna play with and I guess Lamar found out.

"How do you think Luna would feel knowing you had an abortion." My mouth fell open.

How the fuck did he know about that? It happened a long time ago with Marcus. He was my first sexual partner like I stated earlier and the sex was painful in the beginning. Long story short, we had sex unprotected and I popped up pregnant. I never told anyone and went to the abortion clinic to terminate it. I refused to allow Marcus to pressure me into keeping it.

Yes he wanted kids with me but it was early in the relationship and I wanted to finish school.

After the procedure, I told everyone my period was really bad and all I wanted was to be alone. No one thought anything of it and I made sure to start my birth control right away so it wouldn't happen again. Luckily, I did because that punk has two kids during our relationship, which means he was sleeping with both of us unprotected.

"How did you?" I questioned and he gave me the side eye.

"It's my job to know everything, especially; when it comes to my child and since you two were always together, I knew about you as well." I didn't say a word because he is a man who could find out anything, so why am I even surprised?

"I also know about your mom hating you, the fact you tried to commit suicide and you sleeping with the guy who cheated on you. Oh and..."

"I get it Mr. S." I stopped him because he was about to mention everything.

"As far as the abortion, Luna didn't know because she doesn't believe in them. I refused to have someone telling me not to do it."

"A secret is a secret and regardless of her beliefs she would've been there for you." I sat in the truck basking in my own thoughts. He's right but I didn't need to hear, *Are you sure? Does Marcus know? You know it's a sin? Blah, Blah, Blah.*

"So get out your damn feelings and make up because you're gonna need each other if anything happens to your men."

"Say what?"

"Oh this is not some street war where niggas are fighting over a street or county. It's about an entire country, states and the empire alone. People kill for that spot, which is what Oscar will do when he finds out my daughter is married. He's gonna try and do any and everything to destroy it."

"Are you serious?"

"Yes. He's gonna feel like Luna went behind his back and did it on purpose. He'll stop at nothing to be on top and

unfortunately, he has that demon child attempting to help him."
You could hear in his voice how much he despised Julie.

"What you mean?"

"Julie has two kids by Oscar."

"WHAT?" I was shocked.

"Yup. They're young too."

"WOW! If she has kids and Oscar, what does she want
from Luna?"

"Who knows? Julie has been obsessed over hurting
Luna since they were kids. You know that?" I nodded my head.

"If anything, she's only tryna hurt her more by sticking
around. She also knew sleeping with Waleed would basically
make Luna leave him and she loves to witness the hurt."

"Are you sure she's your daughter?"

"I had a test done when she was young to be 100% sure
and unfortunately, she is. What's sad is that, once I kill her, my
wife and I will be the ones raising them."

"I'm lost." He stared out the window for a few minutes.
He just said she had two kids and now he's claiming she's
pregnant again. What is she a baby making machine? I can't

believe he's going to murder his own kid but then again, Julie is definitely on some other shit and always has been.

"Julie is pregnant and supposedly it's Waleed's."

"Oh my God." I covered my mouth. That is gonna kill Luna.

"Luna doesn't know yet but she will be hurt and try to leave Waleed. He's not going to take it well, go on a rampage, and guess who's going with him?"

"Ryan." I whispered to myself.

"Exactly! Ryan. So instead of holding a grudge for the exact same thing you did, suck that pride up and make amends with her."

"Where is she now?"

"Home. Besides there and the mall, where else would she be?" We both got a good laugh off that.

"We're here." The truck stopped.

It appeared to be a warehouse or maybe it's a business. Whatever the case, it was dark and gloomy out here. I knew Mr. S, wouldn't allow anything to happen to me so I wasn't worried about that. This spot had a death feeling to it and all I wanted to do is go back to my car, and then home.

I stepped out and waited for him to finish speaking on the phone. The conversation was in his native language but I've been around them long enough to know what he was saying. Whoever he spoke to knew Lamar was here and must've said he was on his way out because Mr. S, told him, the exact spot where we were sitting.

Imagine my surprise when my fiancé came strolling out looking sexy as shit. I don't know what it is about this man but his ass was perfect to me and the smile on his face could light up any gloomy room. Those eyes mesmerize me every time. Its like they put me in a trance or something.

"Hey sexy. You ok?" He asked and checked me over.

"Yea. What are you doing here?" I asked with an attitude and ready to interrogate him about the photos Lamar showed me. I know, I said, I wouldn't ask but him standing here looking like a snack made my insecurities come out. He was so fine; any woman would want him around her.

"He's a problem I need to get rid of."

29

"Yea well, when you're done we got a problem." He gave me a crazy look.

"What? You think he didn't send me pictures of you and the psycho, crazy bitch Sandy hugging and damn near kissing?"

"What?" He seemed confused.

"You heard me." I stepped away and let them handle their shit because we were definitely going to get to the bottom of those photos. I'm not about to marry a man who's sleeping with someone else. What if she pops up pregnant too? What if she tries to kill me, to get him? All the thoughts had my stomach bubbling and Lord knows, I'm not shitting here. I reached in my purse, grabbed the Prilosec and prayed it helped calm me down.

Risky

When Khloe walked away, I had absolutely no idea what she was talking about. I hadn't seen Sandy since the day she came to Khloe's House poppin shit and fighting her. I almost choked her to death and would've if Waleed didn't stop me. Of course, he came because he knew how I felt about K and Sandy's life was in danger. Lacey is the only other woman I would go to war for and if you knew me, you knew I played no games about my family or woman.

Sandy tried that crying shit and said she was in love with me but I paid her no damn mind. I am fully aware that women become attached faster than men but it's not like I ever discussed her being my woman or that my feelings were involved. Shit, she was there for me to fuck. Nothing more, nothing less and I told her that plenty of times. She just refused to listen and it got her nowhere.

Then, I had this nigga Lamar following Khloe around for some reason. I'm not sure when it started but over the last day or two he's been everywhere she's been but he never approached her, until tonight. I had someone keeping an eye on K, so when he said Lamar was in her face? I told him to get his ass. Luckily, Mr. Suarez, happened to get there first and brought him to me.

Him, myself and Waleed were having a lot of meetings lately to figure out what Oscar was up to and that we needed to prepare ourselves for whatever. He's not gonna take Luna being married and Waleed taking the empire well at all. And to find out him and Julie had two small kids together is crazy. How you betrothed to a woman and have kids with her sister? At least, wait until after you get married and I thought the sister was off limits. I guess this motherfucker felt he could do what he wants.

I lifted the trunk and saw this dumb nigga lying in the back looking like he was ready to cry.

"You just couldn't stay away, could you?" I asked when I drug him out the trunk. His head hit the ground, along with his body.

"FUCK YOU NIGGA! YOU'RE THE REASON MY SISTER IS DEAD AND MY NIECE WAS VIOLATED!" Once he said that, I snapped and started beating the shit outta him. It was like he took me to a place, I tried to stay away from. Who the fuck did he think he was accusing me of allowing bad shit to happen to Raina?

"That's enough Risky. Take him inside and do what you need. We have other important issues to deal with." Mr. Suarez said. I took Lamar by both feet and continued walking in the building. By the time we got in, his shirt was almost over his head and blood was dripping from his back. I guess being scarped up on the ground will do that to you.

"Ryan?" Khloe was standing by the door looking scared.

"Take the keys out my pocket and go sit in my truck." She did like I said and one of the guys followed her. I didn't trust a fucking soul.

One of the guys helped me placed the chains around his ankles and hang him upside down. He was screaming out obscenities one minute, and begging for me to take him down, the next. It's funny how motherfuckers love to test the fuck

outta you but then beg for their life, when it's about to be taken.

Honestly, I should've killed this nigga a long time ago.

He's the one who got Lacey killed and I never forgave him for

it. I'm sure he gave all of you a different story of the actual

event but let me give you a quick rundown.

Lacey was the type of woman who you fell in love with

at first sight. Not only was she beautiful but she had a beautiful

soul and would do anything for you; even give you the clothes

off her back. The people at her job made her employee of the

month one time for a year straight because of who she was. I

thought it was a bit much but we celebrated each time. Lacey

asked me to retire from the drug game so we could raise our

family, travel the world and live happily ever after as she said.

Lamar was the corny brother who wanted to be down

with the game. Lacey never wanted to be around my street life,

which is why I made sure she wasn't. I never answered

business calls around her unless it was the funeral home shit

and if niggas saw us out, they knew not to address me with any of it. I respected the hell outta her for not falling into the gold digger stereotype and promised to give her whatever she wanted.

One day, Lamar called begging Lacey to ask if I could put him on and at first, she didn't ask. It wasn't until I walked in on him yelling at her for not asking and you could tell how upset she was. I had that nigga against the wall fast as hell. I didn't make her cry for shit and I wasn't about to let him do it. She begged me to let him go and that he was sorry. The nigga had the nerve to shake his head yes, like the punk he is. I let go and she told me what happened. It only made me angrier that he went through her instead of coming to me like a man. Hell no, I didn't wanna work with him but let's just say, she knew how to get me to say yes.

Long story short, he was put on and working under Waleed more than anything because I was still in the process of retiring. He wasn't making a lotta money but he made more than others and that's on the strength of him being my girl's brother. He would call Lacey complaining about that too, until I put a stop to that shit. It was like he was never fucking happy.

He was stressing the fuck outta my girl and I was over it. If he did it again after I got in his ass, she never told me.

Anyway, the night I was going to hand the business over to Waleed, Lacey knew and told me to hurry home. I told her she wouldn't be able to contact me for a few hours because the guy didn't like anyone interrupting her meetings. She was well aware of how shit went down, being whenever the guy came to town for meetings it was always the same. Who knew kissing her goodbye that night would be the last time I saw her alive?

We were in the meeting finishing up when I heard someone speaking over the radio about some chick being shot and the guy with her, said it was Risky's girl. I froze at first because there's no way in hell Lacey would come here. I heard the guy speaking again and you could hear Lamar's voice screaming for them to come get me. I jumped up along with Waleed and flew out there, only to find the love of my life dying in front of me. I cried and begged Lacey to stay awake but with each second passing, it was becoming harder to keep her eyes open. The amount of blood leaving her body only verified I was losing her.

The doctors rushed her in the back and not to long after, Waleed told me her mom and Lamar were there. I didn't wanna let his dumb ass in but he talked me into it. I stared at him the entire time waiting to hear from the doctor and then, he was gonna tell me why she was there.

Once the doctor came out hours later giving me the devastating news, I tried to kill him. They had to drag me out the hospital. I wasn't even sure what happened but I knew he was the cause of it, so I went home and checked my cameras. The shit makes me sick to my stomach every time I think about how he sent his sister out there.

"Hello." I watched Lacey pick the phone up while she was in the bedroom getting ready for me to come home. She had on a lingerie set, candles were lit and she looked beautiful.

"I think something happened to Ryan." I could hear him because she had the phone on speaker.

"No, Waleed would've called me." She continued moving around the room preparing it, for when I came in.

"I'm serious Lacey. Word on the street is, Ryan went to the warehouse and shit went bad."

"WHAT?" You could see how frantic she was.

"Yea. I think it was a shootout and then an explosion." She started putting clothes on and told him she had to go find me.

"Lacey, don't leave the house I'll go." We all knew that Lacey acted off impulse whenever she was worried about something. He fucking knew she'd try and come for me.

"No Lamar. I have his phone tracked and it tells me where the warehouse is." I knew all about the tracker because I put it on her phone so she'd always know where I was. That's how I in love with her, I was.

"Stay home sis." He said but not in a demanding way. Its like he knew she'd go and try to save me.

"I just have to see if he's ok."

"Lacey." I could hear him on the phone.

"This stupid bitch is getting on my nerves. LACEY!" He shouted through the phone but it was too late. She had already run out.

That was the last thing on the video before he hung up and Lacey went to find me. It took everyone to hold me back at the funeral because all I wanted was his head. Why would he even bring his ass there, knowing he's the one who had her killed? Sister or not, he had no right to show up. But they say a person who does foul shit, will always show up pretending they had nothing to do with it.

If you're wondering right now why he's not dead it's because dead or not, Lacey loved her brother and I promised never to hurt him. But that shit is long gone now because after he let Veronica get Raina, I knew it was time to get rid of him. Yes, I may have slept with her afterwards but I never allowed her around my daughter.

"Why did you allow Veronica to get Raina?" I had my gun pointed at him.

"My bad Risky. I didn't think she'd do anything at my house." If you're surprised by his statement, you should be. He knew about Veronica bullying and making Raina vomit and still let Ronny around her. He also claimed to kill her if he came in contact with her. So much for that.

39

PHEW! I shot his ass in the leg and listened to him scream.

"Why did you lie to Lacey and say something happened, knowing she would go there?"

"Who told you that?" He questioned. I guess he thought no one knew about his scheme.

"I had cameras in my house, you dumb motherfucker and she had you on speaker." He looked nervous and at first, he didn't answer until I shot him in the other leg.

"Fuck it! You're gonna kill me anyway." He spit blood out and some was dripping down his face from being upside down.

"Why'd you do it?"

"Because."

"Because what nigga?" I kicked him in the stomach.

"You should've turned the empire over to me, instead of Waleed. Since you didn't, I had to take her away from you. I didn't know she'd actually die but oh well."

"Oh well." I had to look and see if he were serious. Did he really admit to getting his sister killed because he was mad at me? What the fuck?

"Your sister loved you."

"Not enough to get you to turn everything over to me."

"You sound stupid. Not that I would but she never even asked."

"I know, which is why I sent her out there. We all know how quick she reacts. It was her stupidity."

"WHAT?"

"You came in her life and she forgot about me. You win and you lose in this life and well, she lost and so did you." I let the rest of my bullets fill his body up. What kind of sick motherfucker gets their own flesh and blood killed over money. I mean they were fucking twins but I guess he had no loyalty to anyone. I stood there staring at his body with thoughts of Lacey's too. Her body didn't have as many bullet holes but one was too much for her.

"You ok?" Waleed asked and took the gun out my hand.

41

"I guess, I found out why he did it. But he could've killed me and not Lacey."

"That nigga was crazy and jealous. Don't blame yourself because you couldn't have predicted any of it."

"I know but why her? She had his niece and I always thought twins looked out for one another." No one said a word as I made my way out the door. I never noticed Khloe come back in. She must've heard everything because there were tears coming down her face. I grabbed her hand and took her to the truck.

"I don't wanna talk about it." She nodded and sat on the driver's side quiet the entire ride home. I'll deal with the other shit she was talking later. Right now, I need a drink and some alone time.

Khloe

After Ryan told me to take the keys out his pocket and go to the truck, I listened. Not because he was bossing me around but because I knew shit was about to get real and I didn't wanna see it. Why did my nosy ass go back in anyway and the moment Lamar started talking, my heart was hurting for Ryan. I can't imagine what he's going through right now.

He did apologize for allowing Raina to be harmed in his care but he had no remorse for setting his sister up. It's like he was happy she died and happier to see Ryan hurting. Was the money and power really worth getting his sister murdered? I guess it was because it's exactly what he did.

After Ryan killed him, no one said a word and sadness was written all over his face. I wanted to hug him or something but the way he held my hand, stopped me. Then he said, he'd deal with the other shit I was talking later. At this point, it no longer mattered because of what he just heard. To know the woman he loved before me, I mean really loved was taken away due to jealousy, is a hard pill to swallow.

I sat quiet the entire ride home but I never let his hand go, until it was time to get in and out the truck. Even when we got to the door, I didn't wanna let go but he said I had to so he could go outside in the back to smoke and be alone.

Instead of bothering him, I went upstairs to shower and get ready for bed. It wasn't really late but my ass was not unpacking any more boxes tonight. We started moving things in here the other day and it's been a lot with Raina being sick and getting things from my house and the one they used to stay in. He had the furniture delivered the day before which is why we were staying here tonight.

After showering and not being able to sleep, I glanced at the time and it was after two in the morning. Ryan wasn't in the bed and it made me worry. I called his phone a few times and it went straight to voicemail. I tossed the covers and ran down the steps and looked everywhere for him but he was gone.

"What's wrong?" I turned around and he was coming out the bathroom with blood shot eyes and his balance was off. I figured he was high and drunk.

"I couldn't sleep and you weren't in the bed." I walked over and placed my hands around his waist. He removed them and sat down.

"I don't feel right sleeping with you right now K." He leaned his head back against the wall and stared at the ceiling.

"Huh?"

"There's another woman on my mind and it would be fucked up laying with you and her in my thoughts."

"WHAT?" I snapped.

"Let me guess. It's Sandy, right? The one you were with earlier."

"Khloe what are you talking about?" He looked at me as if he were really confused.

"I wasn't gonna bring it up but Lamar showed me the photos of you standing there hugging and about to kiss." He chuckled and stood.

"That wasn't me."

"Yes it was. It looked just like you." He came closer to me.

"Khloe, I told you I'd never disrespect you again and I meant it. The last time I saw Sandy was when you beat her ass at your house. I went to see an warn her about ever approaching you again. Whoever that was must resemble me but I was with you and Raina all day and left when Waleed called about some shit."

"Then why..." He lifted my face.

"You played right into the niggas hand K and that shit don't sit right with me." I noticed him grab his keys.

"What?"

"I understand it was a picture and you weren't sure but you should've asked, instead of accusing."

"I..." I tried to speak and he cut me off.

"You believed that motherfucker over me and you don't even know him. Yet, I tell you not to worry about me being with another woman, give you a damn engagement ring, move you in with us and most likely gave you a baby and you still don't trust me."

46

"Ryan."

"Nah Khloe. I get it but what I don't get, is how you accepted all of what I offered when you weren't ready?"

"I am ready."

"No you're not. I told you another woman was on my mind and you automatically assumed it was Sandy."

"Then who was it?" I had my arms folded.

"Lacey."

"Lacey?" I wanted to ask why she was on his mind but after the shut with Lamar, I could figure it out.

"After the shit he revealed, it had my head fucked up. I started reminiscing about the times she and I shared and outta respect for you, I laid on the couch."

"I'm sorry it's just.-"

"I don't wanna hear it." He walked to the door.

"You know Lacey had my heart and no other woman could take me from her. She had my daughter and we were gonna get married." I sucked my teeth because I didn't need to hear that.

"No need to get upset because it's the truth." I stood there looking stupid because I didn't have the right to get mad over a woman before me.

"However, the love I have for you doesn't even compare and you know why?" I remained quiet to hear what he had to say.

"Because my daughter disrespected the shit outta you the first time y'all met, but once she broke down, you still stayed around to make sure she was ok. You let her stay in touch with you, took her out and got her to open up. Something none of us could get her to do. And you did it before knowing I was her father." There was nothing I could say at the moment.

"I fell for you as well but once I found out you were indeed the woman who protected her, my love grew stronger." He looked me in the eye.

"Khloe, you could ask me to murder a hundred people for you and I will. That's how deep in love I am with you." I let the tears roll down my face as he basically told me I fucked up.

"You know, my daughter went through a lot and you were right there on both of our sides. And a nigga is beyond grateful. However, all the love in the world won't make me stay with a woman who don't trust me and takes the word of another man or woman off the street."

"Don't leave Ryan. I'll go. This is your house." He laughed.

"You just don't get it."

"Huh?"

"This house is in both of our names. This is our house and here you are saying, it's mine."

"I just assumed…"

"If you took the time out to stop tryna find things that aren't there, you would see that this is all yours." He took my hand and placed it on his heart.

"No one has it but you." He pecked my lips and walked out the door. All I could do is slide down the wall and cry. How could I believe a man I barely knew, over the one who went through a lot to keep me in his life? He walked out the door and I haven't seen him since.

"Ms. Banks you are four weeks pregnant." The doctor said and showed me, my baby on the screen. Tears flowed down as she pointed out the heartbeat, and anything else she could see.

"Are you ok?"

"Yea. I wish my fiancé was here." I cried because last night after Ryan left, Luna sent me a text asking if I were ok because he was at her house in the extra bedroom. At least he wasn't out with anyone else. It's crazy how we haven't spoken in weeks and she's still in my corner. I never text her back and tried to sleep. It took me a long time but I finally cried myself to sleep.

"Well, I'm setting you up with another appointment in four weeks and hopefully he can make that one." She removed the tube outta me and handed me paper towels to clean up.

When she handed me the prescription paper for prenatal vitamins, I grabbed my things to leave. On the way out, someone bumped into me extremely hard. I looked up and this bitch Sandy, was smirking in my face. I bet she's about to say

Ryan got her pregnant because she's petty like that. Even if she

were, we weren't together at the time so it's nothing I could do.

"What the fuck you looking at?" I laughed at her and

walked out.

"You think you won but I got news for you."

"Sandy, I did win." I flashed my ring and her mouth hit

the floor.

"You see this brand-new Bentley truck I'm driving? It's

courtesy of my fiancé. And the new house he brought is

amazing." When Ryan brought the house, he purchased me a

new truck too. He said now that we're official, he can spoil me

as much as he wants, and that I deserve it after the shit he put

me though in the beginning.

"He only brought you that to make me jealous." This

bitch is really delusional.

"Sandy, I'm gonna find a doctor for you because yo ass

is certified crazy." I hit the alarm on the truck, tossed my purse

inside and went to sit. I felt my hair being pulled and I

should've stopped myself due to the baby in my stomach but

the razor sliding down my face, wouldn't let me. I started beating the shit outta her. Someone pulled me off her and all of a sudden, cops were everywhere.

"Ma'am are you ok? This is officer Richmond. We need an ambulance here." He spoke in the walkie talkie hanging on his shoulder.

"I'm fine."

"Ma'am you have a deep gash coming down your face and it's open." People started coming out the office to be nosy.

A nurse ran over with a thick towel and told me to hold it against my face. I heard the ambulance and asked the cop if he could grab my purse out the truck. Ain't no way in hell I'm getting blood on it.

"Do you need me to call anyone?" The nurse asked and the sad part is, I told her there is no one. At this moment, it's the way I felt and I didn't wanna bother anyone.

"Where's the person who did this?" Now usually I'm no snitch but this bitch is obviously crazy. I searched the parking lot the best I could and she was gone.

"She's not here."

"Do you know why she did this?"

"No. I came out the doctor's office, she said a few words, attacked me from behind and cut me."

"Let's go ma'am." The EMT said and sat me on the stretcher. The cop told me some detectives would look at the tape and try to catch the person who did it.

After the doors closed, I laid my head back and prayed my life would get better and back to normal.

Luna

"Oscar please let me go." I cried out as he held the gun under my chin. When Julie lifted my hand and showed him the ring, I knew it was over. I also knew she was being funny and wanted him to know so he could kill me.

"Are you fucking married?" He asked and there were a few clicks. He threw his arm under my neck and swung me around. Waleed had a gun pointed at his forehead. I could tell he was struggling to pull the trigger, as he should, being Oscar and I were almost the same height. It's no telling if he'd miss and hit me.

"If you don't let my wife go, I'm gonna fucking kill you." Oscar laughed.

"I doubt it." Waleed walked closer and I became nervous.

"Why is that?" Julie appeared to be nervous and made her way behind Oscar.

"Because I have your bitch and from the looks of it, your bastard seed in her stomach."

"And?"

"And, you won't shoot because if you miss, I'm killing her and this kid. If you don't miss and I die, my girl will kill you." I heard another sound and now Julie had a gun out. What the hell is going on?

"Your girl?" I questioned.

"That's right, you stupid bitch. We've been together for a while now and we got two kids together." Julie loved talking shit when she knew I couldn't get to her.

"The way I see it is, you're gonna let me walk outta here or I can kill her and you kill me. Either way you're gonna lose two people. What's it gonna be?" Waleed stood quiet and kept his eyes and gun trained on him. His boys had weapons on Oscar's people and I swear the people at the mall left. It's like the entire place was deserted.

"Yea nigga what's it gonna be?" Julie and Oscar were taunting him.

"Let Luna go and I'll let you walk away. For now."

"Nah, it don't work like that."

"WHAT?" Waleed was pissed.

"I need some leverage so she's coming with me."

"Oh, you got me all the way fucked up." Waleed shouted and I heard a shot go off. Julie screamed.

"Waleed how are you gonna shoot me in my leg, when I'm carrying your child?" It was at that moment I remembered her saying that she was pregnant by my husband. The tears started to roll down my face as Oscar still had a grip on me.

"My wife is the only one having my kid."

"Think again Wale. We fucked a lot and like any woman looking to get paid, I poked holes in the condom." Oscar sucked his teeth.

"That nigga got money. You did this to hurt her." Waleed went back and forth with my sister, as if Oscar didn't still have his gun on me.

"Sure did and I'm keeping it." Some guy lifted her up and carried her to a black truck.

Oscar walked backwards and basically dragged me with him. Guns were still drawn and tempers were running high. All I could think of was my husband being stupid because he was mad and now there would be a demon spawn coming from my sister for him.

Once we got to the truck, some guy hopped in the driver's seat, started it and pulled off at the same time Oscar threw me to the ground and I caught myself from hitting my stomach but my knee was fucked up. I couldn't even get up and the throbbing started instantly.

"Fuck! You ok? Shit, you have to go to the hospital." Waleed came over to me looking stressed out.

"GET THE FUCK OFF ME!" I shouted and noticed his friends turning their heads.

"Luna?"

"Is it a possibility that Julie is pregnant by you?" He ran his hand down his face and remained quiet. Its like he had to think hard and that alone pissed me off.

"I want this marriage annulled." He laughed this cynical laugh, kneeled down next to me and put his mouth by my ear.

"I fucked up and you could be mad forever but ain't no annulling shit."

"You heard what I said Waleed. We are over." He yanked my hair back.

"Yo. Waleed." I heard Risky say. It was so many of his people here, I didn't even see Risky at first.

"And you heard what the fuck I said. Go down to the courthouse and I'll chop your fucking hands off before they hand you a pen to sign papers." My eyes got big. He's always threatening me and I knew it was just talk but the way he looked right now, had me petrified.

"My boy is gonna take you to the hospital and I'll be home later." Risky and Waleed lifted me up and helped me in the truck.

"You can't make me stay married to you." I closed the door and locked it but the damn window was down. So much for talking shit and leaving.

"I beg to differ."

"It's over Waleed." He was getting angrier.

"And I said it's not."

"Waleed, I don't wanna leave you but another baby? Really?"

"Just let me explain Luna."

"There's nothing to explain. You were that fucking mad at me and put a fucking baby in her? I hate you. I FUCKING HATE YOU. I HATE YOU. I HATE YOU." I screamed out and kept punching him in the face and chest through the window and not once did he stop me.

"Luna."

"DON'T SAY MY NAME. PLEASE JUST LEAVE ME ALONE!" I was now hysterical crying. Risky told the guy to pull off because Waleed was tryna get the door opened.

"LUNA!" I rolled the window up and cried like a baby.

When we pulled up to the hospital, the driver ran in and had a nurse bring a chair out. A tech came out with her and helped me get out. They asked how far along I was and took me straight upstairs. They took me for x-rays and hooked me up to the machine to check on the baby. After telling me my knee was fractured, they placed a brace on it and told me I need to see an orthopedic.

I had to stay there for two hours because the doctor wanted to make sure my son was ok. He printed out a 3D picture for me and I was pissed. Even in my stomach he resembled his ugly ass father.

The nurse came in not too long after with the discharge papers for me to sign and a wheelchair to take me downstairs. I called my mom and told her I was taking an Uber there and explain what happened. I could hear my father going off in the background. I hung up and asked the nurse to leave me outside. I wanted to be alone. At first, she wouldn't do it but once I got out the chair and sat on the bench she said fuck it.

"Khloe?" I shouted and she turned around. I only knew it was her because for some reason, her ugly ass mom was standing outside the car. When she turned to see who called her, there was a bandage covering one side of her face. I could see her mother roll her eyes.

"What?" She answered and stood to leave.

"Are you ok? What happened to your face? Where's Risky?" I glanced around to see if he was coming out. He slept at my house the other day so I figured they were arguing. But if she's here with a bandage on her face, he can't be too far away.

"I'm fine. What happened to you?" She pointed to my leg.

"It's a long story but in short terms, Oscar is in town, tried to kill me but Waleed showed up. Oh, and I want my marriage annulled."

"You want a divorce already?" I could tell she was confused.

"Julie announced she's pregnant by my husband and he basically told me I can't annul the marriage." I shrugged my shoulders.

"WOW! You really wanna leave him?"

"I don't wanna raise a kid he's having with her and I won't."

"I can't argue with that. What are you gonna do?"

"Let's go Khloe." Her mom yelled before I got to answer and got in the car.

"She still a bitch?"

"Ain't nothing change but the weather. Do you have a ride?" I was shocked to hear her ask.

"I'm waiting on an Uber."

"An Uber. Luna you don't take cabs." I had to laugh because she's right.

"You do when all your bodyguards were shot in front of you."

"Oh my God." She covered her mouth.

"Yea. I had a pretty hectic day."

"Same here. Come on." She walked over to help me stand and handed me the stupid crutches.

"Your mom is gonna have a fit. You know she can't stand me and you're bringing me to get a ride."

"She'll be alright."

"Huh?" I asked because usually she would ask her mom first and go back and forth before shutting down. Now, its like she doesn't care.

"After I almost choked her to death, she doesn't really bother me anymore."

"WHATTTTTT?"

"I'll tell you at the house."

"I can't wait to hear this shit." She laughed.

"Can you do me a favor and shut your phone off?"

"I already did because I don't wanna talk to him." She

nodded, closed the door for me and her mom drove in silence.

It was refreshing not to be arguing with me. I did turn my

phone back on to send my mom a text and tell her, I'd call

tomorrow. She was a worry wart but she's still my mom.

I shut the phone off when she responded and let my

head rest on the seat. A little while later we pulled up to her

mom's. Khloe thinks she slick. She knew Ryan would never

look for her over here but shit my soon to be ex-husband

wouldn't think to look here either so I'm all for it.

We got out and her mom left us and went in the house.

After we stepped in, both of us went to the extra bedroom and

started telling each other what happened. I felt bad for her

because Ryan is really in love with her and she should've

never listened to Lamar. I also felt bad for Ryan. That had to

be hard to hear. I told her my drama and she couldn't believe it.

"Khloe I wanna say I'm so sorry for not inviting you to the shotgun wedding and not telling you about the baby. I swear it wasn't intentional. It was last minute, Waleed grabbed me out the club and said most likely you were coming with Ryan. He text Ryan but he said you were drunk and he took you home. I thought he told you but I guess not. I'm so sorry. You know you're my sister and I would never purposely leave you out. Do you forgive me?"

"Yea. If you ever do that again I won't ever speak to you. And stop threatening my step daughter." I busted out laughing.

"She's a got damn snitch. I guess Ryan told you too?"

"No. I had to make him tell me. By the way, thanks for the outfit and whatever else you helped him with."

"How was it? Did you take pictures? I wish we could've been there but you hated me at the time."

"I didn't hate you, its just you should've told me."

"I know and again, I'm sorry." She and I hugged it out.

"Waleed told me, Risky asked you to marry him." She grabbed her purse and took the ring out. It was humongous.

"Why don't you have it on?" She shrugged.

"I don't think he wants to marry me now so I took it off at the hospital."

"Why you say that?"

"After the things he said, I saw it in his face." She started crying and laid down.

"He's gonna marry you Khloe. He just needs time right now and you have to stop listening to others. Ryan has never lied to you so I'm sure he would've told you the truth whether it hurt or not." She wiped her face.

"How many stitches did you get?" She removed the bandage a little and I have to say, Sandy really did a number on her. The entire right side of her face, close to ear was sliced. They gave her thirty-five stitches and told her she may need plastic surgery to cover the scar.

"Why did you call your mom if y'all weren't speaking?" I had to know the answer to that.

"Because I know no one would look for me here. I mean if they were, this is the last place they'd think I was at." She said and stood to get in the shower.

On the way here, we stopped at Walmart and the two of them went in to grab a few things. Some pajamas for us, a few pair of leggings, T-shirt's, underclothes, toothbrushes and anything else she thought we needed.

"Goodnight Khloe and thanks for being my sister again."

"Goodnight Luna and don't let it happen again." She turned the television off and both of us were knocked out. I guess with everything going on, sleep found us quickly. Hopefully, my dumb ass husband won't.

Oscar

"How the fuck is that bitch pregnant and married? Who the fuck approved that shit? Where is the agreement because this shit can't be right?" I shouted out to no one in particular.

"Calm down Oscar." I looked over at Julie and smiled. She was lying in the hotel bed with my ten-month-old son on her chest and my two-year-old daughter was next to them. The nanny was in the room down the hall. These three were the reason I woke up every day.

To be honest, I had enough money to last two lifetimes and didn't need the empire my father was tryna get me to take. I spoke to him years ago about relinquishing my involvement in it but he refused. He said, men don't go back on their word. I had to ask, how can I go back on something that was done prior to my knowledge? At the time, I was thirteen so he smacked the fuck outta me for talking back. Saying me questioning him, is disrespectful. Shit, I think making someone do something they didn't really want to, was just as disrespectful.

Over the years, he began to groom me for this so-called takeover. Mind you, I've only been to America a few times in my life so I had no idea what I was stepping into. Needless to say, he had me making secret trips over here for reasons unknown to me. I could care less because it gave me time with Luna, who I did fall for in the beginning. She was a little thick but her personality was the shit and she was funny as hell. We were like best friends but once we had sex, everything changed. I was the second guy she ever had sex with and I must say whoever taught her, did a good ass job because any woman who can make you say her name, is the shit.

My father found out and pressured me to get her pregnant. Luna and I never had unprotected sex so when I tried she stopped me. Being we were friends she asked what the sudden change and when I told her, she snapped. It was as if she turned into another person. She started cursing me out and claiming to never wanna see me again. I ain't gonna lie, that shit hurt my feelings because I was already in love with her.

She stopped taking my calls and refused to come see me or let me see her.

Anyway, the hurt in me, had me saying mean and hurtful things to her. I would say things like, she needed to lose weight because she'd get fatter when we had kids and a bunch of other shit. Hell yea, she cried and sadness was always written over her face but I didn't care. If you hurt me, I was going to do my best to return the favor.

After not seeing each other anymore and barely talking, someone brought Julie to me and asked for her to work at the strip club I owned. She was skinny, nervous and beautiful. I asked if she were a virgin and once she said yes, that was it. I made her my woman, forbid her to strip and took care of her.

Unfortunately, I cheated a few times on her and she left me. Sad to say, she ended up with that nigga Waleed and at first, I didn't care. But when she called to tell me about them expecting, I knew then if I didn't get her back now, she'd never come home. I made her terminate it and we've been going hard ever since.

If you really wanna know, she's the other reason I'm coming for the empire. She feels like its owed to her. After her pops killed her mom and he kicked her out with nothing, which is how she ended up with me, she wanted revenge. I wanted to feel bad but once my father told me the real reason her pops kicked her out and Luna hated her, I had to agree that she was fucked up. But it doesn't stop me from loving her. Shit, she didn't do me wrong and she ain't nowhere near crazy to even attempt to try some crazy shit. I let it be known from the gate, how things were gonna be and we've never had an issue.

"How can you ask me to be calm, when your sister married him and pregnant? You do know, unless there's a clause in that agreement, you won't get the empire."

"With him thinking this baby is his, even if he has it, he'll have to share it with the mother of his child." I looked over and my kids were asleep on the bed. I snatched her up by the hair.

"Oscar! My leg." I glanced down and remembered Wale shot her for running her mouth.

"Fuck that leg. You were supposed to make her think y'all slept together, not really do it." I was pissed because the plan was to make believe she slept with him so it would tear Luna and Waleed apart. When she mentioned the baby could be his, I was pissed but played it off well. I couldn't let them know we weren't on the same page.

"I'm sorry Oscar. It was the only way to get close to him."

"You know that's a fucking lie. How many times did you sleep with him?" I left her here for a week to go check on some things in Mexico. Its no telling what she was doing.

"Oscar." She had tears running down her face.

"HOW MANY?" I screamed and she jumped. My kids stirred in their sleep a little but didn't wake up.

"The week you were gone, we had sex a few of those days." I punched her hard as hell in the face. Her lip split open and when I dropped her, she let out a high-pitched scream.

"I told you not to fuck him. What you missed his dick or something?"

"No Oscar. Stop!" I started kicking her in the stomach and back.

"Is that really my baby? You dumb bitch. How could you?" My anger got the best of me and I literally beat the crap outta her. My kids were yelling because she was screaming but had no idea what was going on. I opened the door and my bodyguard was outside the door.

"Take this bitch to the hospital and have them check to see if she miscarried. If she didn't, take her ass to the fucking clinic to terminate it." I kneeled down next to her.

"There better not be a baby in your stomach when you get back. Do I make myself clear?"

"Yes." She said barely above a whisper.

"Get her the fuck out my face." He lifted her up and I grabbed my son who almost rolled off the bed and picked my daughter up with my other arm. I rocked them back to sleep, laid them down and opened up my laptop. If that nigga thought for one second, he would have a kid by Julie, he was sadly mistaken.

****

"What's going on over there?" My father asked. I hadn't spoken to him since finding out about Luna's pregnancy.

"Evidently, the agreement is null and void."

"How is that?" He asked and I glanced over at Julie who was balled up on the bed. Its been two weeks since she miscarried and her face is starting to clear up.

"Luna is already married and expecting."

"WHAT?" He shouted on the phone and went on and on about how everything should automatically be mine since she broke the agreement. I had to remind him about Julie and his two grandkids. He told me it doesn't count because we're not married.

"Pops, I don't know what to tell you." Julie sat up and stared at me. She knew if I was on the phone with my father it wasn't good. It never is.

"You don't have to tell me shit. What you're gonna do is take the empire from them."

"How is that? Matter of fact, I don't even want it." I heard Julie suck her teeth.

"Son, I didn't sign this shit for you to say fuck me. That is my fucking empire he stole from me and I want it back." My father told me a hundred times that Luna's father and him were partners some years ago. My dad got locked up and her dad found another partner because he wasn't taking the chance of doing any business through the jails and end up in the same place. It made sense and her dad, picked his brother to work alongside of him.

When he was released from prison, he wanted his spot back and Luna's pops said no. He's been salty ever since. Luna's father did offer the empire to me through the agreement, which is why he's so mad. He's under the impression that if I have it, I'd give it to him. I don't have a problem doing that but is it really that serious? My pops is old as hell and should be retired and relaxed somewhere.

"Now either you're gonna take it voluntarily or I'm gonna take those fucking kids from you and you'll never see them again." He was so loud Julie heard him and covered her mouth.

My father isn't one of those people where you took his threats lightly. If he said something, he meant it. Did I want him to take my kids? What would he do with them, if he did? I couldn't take the chance and told him what he wanted to hear. I had to come up with a plan and fast, otherwise; I'd have to disappear with my family and who wants to live paranoid for the rest of their life? I hung the phone up and looked at Julie.

"What are you gonna do?"

"I guess get rid of Waleed."

"Oscar, maybe we should leave and never come back." She shocked the hell outta me with that statement.

"Wait! I thought you wanted this empire."

"I did but if it involves bringing harm to my babies, then forget it." I pulled her down on my lap and made love to her mouth with mine.

"You ready to get this shit over with?" I smacked her on the ass.

"Let's figure out something quick so we can leave. I don't trust your father."

"Me neither."

Waleed

When Luna sent me a text saying, Julie approached her outside the mall, I hopped in my truck with Risky and flew over there. In route, he hit up some of the crew and told them to meet us. Not knowing if Oscar would show up, we had to be sure there were enough of us, as them.

I wasn't too worried because Luna always had protection around. Unfortunately, when we pulled up the guards were on the ground and this nigga had a gun under my wife's chin. I was beyond pissed and if you know me, you know that wasn't gonna fly.

It took me all of five seconds to get out and point my gun at Oscar. He had Luna crying and I saw her stomach clear as day, which means he did too. Her shirt was covering her but you knew she was carrying my kid.

My gun was still pointed on his head as him and dumb ass Julie started popping shit. I put a bullet in her leg and waited for Oscar to make the slightest move so I could take him out. At this very moment, I wish I had my laser gun because I wouldn't be so worried about missing him and hitting Luna. His ass would be on the ground already.

Oscar's punk ass had the nerve to drag my wife with him to the truck to keep me from shooting him. After he got in and pushed Luna to the ground, everyone started shooting. There were bullet holes on the side of his truck but it could be bulletproof for all we know and it's no guarantee anyone got hit.

But the worst part about all of this, is Luna asking to get the marriage annulled. She is my wife and I'm not about to let her go through with it. Plus, I only planned on being married once in my life so she's stuck, whether she likes it or not.

"You think she really gonna leave?" I asked Risky who was going through his own shit with Khloe. I told him it's his fault she's insecure but I also understand his point of her believing people she didn't know. It's gonna take them a minute to get it right too.

"She's mad and hurt right now. How you get shorty pregnant though?" We both sipped on the beer at the club. Hell yea we were here, I needed a drink. I'll look for her in an hour or so in order to give her time to cool off.

"It's probably hurting more because it's her sister. The one who tried to kill her mom and now her. She probably all fucked up in the head right now." He said making me think about how fucked up the situation really is.

"Man, I don't think it's my kid." I told him honestly because I don't believe it is.

"I'm lost bro."

"Check this out." I turned my seat all the way around to look at the strippers who came out.

"I'm extra, extra careful when I fuck a chick, drunk or not." It wasn't a lie. Bitches are scandalous as fuck and like I always say, I'm not having a bunch of baby mamas.

"I'm no fool and Julie can say she put holes in the condom all she wants but her dumb ass forgot, I'm the one who opened the brand-new boxes, I brought. Was I drunk a few times? Absolutely! But never drunk where I'm tryna have a bunch of kids." He nodded and turned to look at the stripper who tapped his shoulder. These women were bad as hell but not to make me cheat on my wife. I had enough problems when I was mad and slept with Julie. I don't need those type of issues again.

"Hey Ryan." We both turned around and it was Sandy and some chick.

"What the fuck you want?" He had no problem talking to her like shit.

"You." He looked her up and down before smirking. Sandy had on a short ass dress with some boots up her thigh and her titties were about to fall out the dress.

"Is that right?" Her friend moved closer to me and I can admit she too, was bad.

"Risky why you doing me like this?" She wrapped her hands around his neck and I thought he was gonna kill her by how hard he threw them off.

"Yo, why you got all that makeup on?" I shouted and Ryan turned to look at her. He grabbed her chin and examined her face. The few times I was around her, I've never noticed any makeup on her face. Now, she had on so much it looked caked on.

"Were you in a fight?" She didn't answer and rolled her eyes.

"Oh, that fat bitch didn't tell you?" Ryan stood and I had to get in front of him.

"Call her fat one more time."

"Risky you too fine to be with her. Why can't you see I'm the one?" I never understood why women couldn't move on when a man said, he had someone else.

"Did you touch my fiancé?" When he said that, I had to look at Sandy because he already warned her not to go around Khloe.

"She attacked me at the doctor's office. What I'm not supposed to defend myself?" She said it in a non chalant way but my boy wasn't tryna hear it.

"What doctors office?" He moved past me and had her yoked up by the throat.

"I'm pregnant and..." He dropped her on the floor.

"I'm not even gonna entertain that shit because we both know it's not mine but if Khloe tells me a different story, I promise to find and kill you." He hock spit in her face.

80

"RYAN!" She shouted and wiped her face. Is this bitch serious? Who gets spit on and still goes after the person?

"Yo, you nasty." I said and followed him out the club.

"Man fuck her. She lucky that's all I did." He pulled his phone out and put it to his ear.

"You talked to Luna?" He asked and jumped in the car.

"Nah. Her phone off but her mom said she's ok and resting.

"Fuck! Khloe phone is off too. I swear if anything happened to her, I'm gonna kill Sandy."

"Did you go to the house?"

"I'm about to. You want me to drop you off?"

"Hell yea nigga. You out yo rabid ass mind, if I'm going to the house and y'all make up, then I have to listen to moaning. No thanks. Take my black ass home." He started laughing hard as hell but I was dead serious. Those two couldn't keep their hands off each other and I'll be damned if I listen to them act like porn stars and my wife ain't giving it up.

****

"Yo. What's good?" I asked Dora who was standing at the gate of my house when Risky dropped me off.

"I miss you Wale. Why can't we be together?" What is this, try and fuck yo ex week? These bitches coming outta nowhere.

"Bitch, you miss this dick cuz yo nigga gone." I blew weed smoke in her face.

"That's not it Waleed. You know I'm in love with you." I laughed at her dumb ass.

"In love, huh?" She stood there with a sad look on her face.

"Were you in love when you upgraded your family with my money? Or when you started sleeping with Lamar thinking it would hurt me? Or the fact you knew what Ronny was doing to my niece?"

"I swear, I never knew she did that to Raina. I loved Raina as if she were my own niece and I'm sorry she went through that. Wale, you know damn well I'm not the type of person who would've let that fly."

"I don't have a clue as to what type of person you are. Shit, you've done so much its hard to tell." She sucked her teeth.

"What you want Dora because I know for a fact you didn't come all this way to say hi." I gave her a fake smile and waited. She was twiddling her thumbs like a kid about to get in trouble.

"I'm pregnant and Lamar is probably dead and gone."

"What does that have to do with me?" She placed her hands on my chest.

"Bitch, bye." I pushed them off and turned to go in.

"Wale, I need your help."

"With what?"

"Lamar didn't leave me any money; his mother hates me and I have nowhere to go."

"And you're telling me this because…"

"Wale, you may be with that other chick but I know you still have love for me. Can you help me get a spot until I get on my feet?"

"WHAT? I'm not your man."

"I know but I have nowhere else to go."

"You better stay in a shelter. Why can't you go with yo raggedy ass mama?" She sucked her teeth.

"Wale, please." She stood there begging and whining for a good two minutes. My brain was telling me don't do shit for her but the little bit of love I had left, wouldn't allow me to let her live on the street.

"I'll set you up in one of the apartments Risky has but that's it. I ant giving you no money, no food, clothes, nothing. Got it." She let a smile come on her face.

"But how am I supposed to live?"

"Not my problem. Lets go." I had her get in the passenger side of my ride and took her to the four-family house Risky had. He rented it out but there was a one bedroom available. I used it from time to time if I didn't feel like driving home. Hell, he did too when he wanted to be away from Veronica.

We got there and I opened the door. Her eyes grew big because the place was fully furnished, there was cable, food and a house phone inside. She walked around and had the nerve to offer up some fucking pussy.

"I don't want none of that stinking, rotten, garbage pussy you've been giving away. My wife more than satisfies me."

"Your wife."

"That's right bitch. My wife." I showed her my ring and her eyes started watering.

"Get your life Dora."

"What? I wish it was me."

"Well it ain't and never will be so stop wishing. Now like I said, I ain't giving you shit and if you cause any problems over here, you're on your own. Peace." I went to leave and the bitch had the nerve to jump up and kiss me. The force from my hand pushing her back, caused her to fall and I gave zero fucks.

"YO! Don't ever out your dirty, crusty, canker sore, infected ass lips on me again." She started crying.

"Bye." I didn't apologize or even ask if she were ok. In my eyes, she's lucky I gave her dirty ass somewhere to stay.

And even though I did, it doesn't mean put your lips on mine. These bitches are really crazy. Let me take my ass home so I can be fully rested before bringing my wife back. Me and her are gonna be locked in the room for a long ass time after this.

Sandy

"Oh my God Sandy. That shit is nasty as hell." My friend Reesy/ co-worker said as she stood there watching me get up off the floor. The tramp didn't hand me a napkin or her hand.

"He's upset right now. He'll be ok." I walked over to the bar, picked up a few napkins and wiped my face. A few women were staring and pointing and the bartender shook her head.

"WHAT?" I shouted.

"Don't get mad at me because Risky almost took your life." She had the nerve to say and in a sarcastic tone. She had no idea what she was talking about.

"What the fuck ever." I waved her off and she tapped my shoulder.

"Look here honey." She threw the rag on the bar and came around to where I was.

"I don't know who you are, nor do I give a fuck but what you won't do is bring your high sadity ass in here talking shit."

"Excuse me." I had my hand on my hip and Reesy stood there watching. She's nowhere near scary but with these other women surrounding us, it didn't look like it would be a fair fight.

"Risky isn't the type of guy who will continue to let you stalk him."

"STALK?" I questioned.

"Yea bitch, STALK. You know show up where he is uninvited, fuck with his woman or any family member. Then you're in here being desperate and tryna fuck, when all of us in here knows he won't ever give you or any other woman the time of day."

"Yea ok. I've had him already."

"Exactly! You had him and he must've dissed your ass because you're in here tryna get him to take you home. Honey, he is very happy with his fiancé." I sucked my teeth. I guess the fat bitch wasn't lying about her being engaged.

"Why do you even care? What? You fucking him too?" She chuckled and before I knew it, we were going at it in the club. She definitely got a few good hits but so did I.

"Yo! Whoever you are. You gotta go." The security guard said and snatched me up. I was almost walking on my tippy toes from the way he had my dressed bunched up in his hand. I tried to keep the bottom half of my dress down but it was no use. I could feel the air on my ass cheeks.

"Don't bring your ass back here." He pushed me hard as hell.

"Girl you crazy." Reesy shook her head.

"Really! You didn't even get in it." I pulled my dress down and attempted to get it together, when deep down all I wanted to do is cry. Why was Ryan treating me this way and did this Khloe bitch really have his heart?

"One... it was a one on one fight and two... bitch you are a fucking doctor. A psychologist! What the fuck are you doing making a fool of yourself over a nigga who obviously doesn't want you?" I ignored her comment because she didn't know shit.

"If you continue being this reckless, you're gonna lose everything. Is he worth it?" I sat in the driver's side of my car and stared in the darkness. Did I want to lose everything? Is he worth it?

****

It's been two days since the bullshit happened at the club the other night. I text and called Ryan until he blocked me. I called from different numbers and once he heard my voice he'd hang up. I even stopped by his house and noticed it was empty. Again, I guess Khloe wasn't lying about him buying her a house. Now I'm sitting here at work, canceling appointments because he clouded my mind so bad, I couldn't focus.

I don't know why I'm obsessing over Ryan. Yes, I said it. I'm obsessed. I guess it's because he's not your average hood nigga. Don't get me wrong, I've witnessed his anger a few times and I'm sure it can be worse but underneath, he's a sweetheart. Not only can he do amazing things to my body but the love he has for his daughter is commendable. Something about the way he values their relationship as father and daughter makes me want to have his child just to see it.

As you can see, I tried the pregnant line with him like most women and he saw right through that. He'd wear a condom and pull out before he came. I thought he would forget or something but nope. And now the fat bitch walked out the doctor's office with that blue prescription paper in her hand. I knew it was the prescription for prenatal vitamins because what else would it be for? They don't give you those sheets for an appointment.

Hell yea, I fought her. I wanted to kick that damn baby right out her stomach but she protected it well. She gave me the business and that's why I sliced her face. Let's see if Ryan is gonna wanna layup with scar face now.

"I don't wanna come back. I'm fine." I heard a voice in one of the offices that appeared to be Raina's. I peeked in Reesy's office and sure enough it was her. Ryan had her stop coming to me after I questioned Khloe in my office, the first time we met. Anyone could see the love she had for him but I made sure to let her know Ryan was mine. Unfortunately, they stayed together.

"Honey, I know you don't want to be here but your father thinks you should come more and honestly, so do I." I stood outside the door to see what Raina's response would be. I was shocked to see her father wasn't with her. Then again, it could be a private session.

"Why do I need to come? The woman and my uncle can no longer bother me, so what's the use?" I stepped in the office. Raina looked up, sucked her teeth and rolled her eyes.

"Its in your best interest to stay in counseling."

"Ms. Preston, what are you doing here?" Reesy asked.

"I was walking by and overheard the conversation. Being as I used to counsel her, I just thought maybe I could shed some light on the situation."

"On what? My dad said you're unprofessional, which is why I don't come see you anymore." Reesy looked at her and then me. I never told her why he asked her to see another counselor and she must not have put two and two together.

"Unprofessional, says the man who was sleeping with me and the fat bitch." I gave Raina a fake smile and she smirked. If I could smack the shit outta her, I would.

"Ms. Preston, you are way out of line." Reesy stood up and gave me the look of death. It was in my best interest to leave but I couldn't. My feet were stuck and I needed to say, what was on my mind to this little heffa.

"Oh really! Did this little bitch tell you her father killed the woman molesting her and most likely the uncle too? Huh? Did she tell you that?" I found myself getting angrier.

"Ms. Preston, why are you so upset? Is it because my dad didn't choose you? He fell for a woman who can relate to a child more than a counselor? Or that he's engaged and loving the hell outta my future stepmother? I mean its the only reason I can come up with as to why you're upset." Raina said with a smirk on her face.

"You fucking bitch."

WHAP! I smacked the shit outta her.

"OH MY GOD! ARE YOU FUCKING CRAZY? SECURITY! SECURITY!" Reesy yelled and pulled me away from Raina.

"My daddy must have you strung out but guess what?" She moved closer.

"Once he hears about this, you're gonna be hanging from a string." Reesy looked at her and then me.

"Matter of fact, I may ask if he'll allow me to watch what he does to you. You're a pathetic piece of shit and my dad should have never fucked you." No the fuck she didn't.

"I'm gonna fucking kill this little bitch." I got away from Reesy and ran over to her.

Psssssss! Psssssss! Psssss! Psssssss! Is all I heard and found myself choking. The bitch sprayed the hell outta me with mace.

"What's going on in here?" My boss and a few security people ran in the office.

"This woman attacked me. Look at my face." My boss and security looked and there was a huge handprint on it. I knew then my job was gone and finished going off.

"Ms. Preston, what were you thinking?" Security was trying to calm me down.

"This little bitch just sprayed me with mace."

"HOW DARE YOU CALL THIS CHILD A NAME?" My boss yelled out and Raina was smiling again.

"Fuck her and her father. I'm gonna make sure the two of you suffer." Security now had me in their arms, one on each side.

"Is that a threat Ms. Preston? My dad would not be happy to hear about this." She was getting a kick outta this shit.

"You may have gotten away from the other woman, but you won't get away from me." I saw Raina's facial expression change and so did everyone else's. I didn't mean to say it but she was tainting the hell outta me.

"MS. PRESTON, YOU KNOW BETTER THAN TO THREATEN A CHILD. WHAT IS WRONG WITH YOU?" My boss shouted and outta nowhere, Raina's grandmother came in.

"Raina, are you ok?" She asked as the security people began to escort me out the room.

95

"I'm fine nana. This woman smacked me and tried to attack me. I sprayed her with mace."

"Oh she did huh?" It didn't take long for her to hit me and once she did, the entire place was in an uproar. People were trying to get her off me but she had my hair extra tight. I'm not sure but I felt a few kicks on the other side of me and I bet they came from Raina.

"This is for smacking me bitch." When her foot made contact with my face, I swear a bitch saw stars. Whatever sneakers she had on, did a number on me and I was ready to pass out.

"Break it up. Break it up." I looked and there were a bunch of cops. They pulled us apart and placed handcuffs on me and Raina's grandmother.

"Ms. Preston, you are fired. Please don't return here after you leave the precinct. Anything you have will be delivered to your house." My boss said and pulled Raina away.

"But?"

"You are no longer allowed in this building and if you attempt to come inside, you will be arrested again." I put my head down and allowed the cops to escort me out.

"Nana, daddy said he's gonna come get me and meet you at the station." When Raina yelled that out, its like my stomach automatically went in knots. He's going to fucking kill me.

Risky

"What you mean nana is getting arrested?" I asked Raina on the phone. I was on my way to Khloe's mom house to see her. Its been a few days and she hasn't come home, called or even sent me a text message.

I went to see her dad, assuming she was there and he told me she was with her mom, which shocked the hell outta both of us. He said, she told him how she messed up with me and planned on giving me space. Truth is, I didn't need space. Yes, she pissed me off but it doesn't make me wanna live without her. I hurt her in the beginning, therefore; I know it will be hard for her to trust me. But, I also won't be in a relationship where every time I leave the house she thinks something or believes anyone off the street before asking me.

"I was in my therapy session and Ms. Preston came in." I specifically told Sandy and her boss on two separate occasions, she is not to have any meetings with Raina or to even sit in on one. She was unprofessional and couldn't keep her hate for Khloe in the closet. I didn't want her badgering my daughter with questions about K either and knowing now the type of person Sandy is, I'm positive she would have.

"WHAT?" I yelled through the phone.

The day Khloe came in to sit on the meeting, Sandy was definitely in her feelings. She started the meeting off fine but then she began asking Khloe questions like, *how close are you and her father? Do you two have alone time? Will you be coming over often? I had to stop her when she asked if we were ever intimate with one another.* Raina was there and it was inappropriate as fuck.

I swore Khloe was gonna kill her and had her step outside so I could talk to Sandy. That next day, I called Sandy's boss but didn't go into detail about why I no longer wanted her services. Sandy appeared to be a great counselor but her feelings got in the way of her work.

Needless to say, they transferred Raina to a different woman and my daughter seemed to like her. I figured her boss would inform her not to allow Sandy in on her sessions as well but maybe she didn't.

Yesterday she called and asked if Raina could come in separate. She claims that children speak more freely when a parent isn't there and I agreed. I dropped her off and my mom was picking her up because we were still dealing with finding Oscar. Waleed was losing his damn mind because Luna wouldn't speak to him so shit was fucked up all around. Had I known this sneaky bitch would attempt to sit in on her session, I never would've left.

"Yea, she smacked me and…" I cut her off.

"Come again. I know damn well you didn't say she put her hands on you."

"Yes she did daddy and tried to do it again but I had the mace Ms. K gave me. I sprayed her a whole bunch of times, then I kicked her in the face when nana had her on the ground." I smiled when she mentioned K. I appreciated her teaching my daughter how to protect herself.

"Nana was fighting?"

"Yup. She beat her ass too dad, which is why they arrested her." I wanted to tell Raina to stop cursing but I could tell how upset she was and gave her a pass.

100

"I'll be there in a minute to get you and then we'll go get nana." She hung up and I told her to wait inside. I hung up and dialed Khloe again. She still wasn't answering but I had a trick for that ass later.

I pulled up in front of the therapist office and noticed cops and two ambulances. People were sitting inside getting those oxygen masks put on their face. I guess Raina lit the entire office up with the mace.

"Where's my daughter?" I ran over to the cops and one pointed in the office. I walked in and noticed EMT people assisting a few workers. Raina was in the corner texting away on her phone.

"Raina!" She looked up and came towards me.

"Mr. Wells, can I speak to you?" Raina's therapist asked. I walked in with my daughter behind me. I'll be damned if she stays out here alone. She closed the door and offered us a seat.

"Mr. Wells, please accept my apology for what took place here."

"I need to know what the fuck happened." She looked nervous and I gave zero fucks.

"Your daughter and I, were in a session and Ms. Preston came in, uninvited I might add."

"How did she know Raina was here and why was the door opened? I thought sessions are closed."

"Raina claimed to feel claustrophobic with the door closed and asked if she could open it. Ms. Preston must've overheard us speaking. Unfortunately, she walked in and let's just say, things got out of control."

"Step outside for a minute Raina and close the door." I didn't want her to be alone but I needed to know everything.

"Don't leave from in front of this door." She nodded and closed it.

"What you mean let's just say things got outta control." I walked over to her desk and placed my gun at her temple.

"Tell me in motherfucking detail what happened and why my fucking daughter was attacked by a grown ass woman in a place, she's supposed to feel safe at?" The woman started crying and told me the entire story.

"I see." I put my gun in my waist and moved back.

"Just so you know, I will be seeking elsewhere for my daughter to receive therapy."

"Mr. Wells, Ms. Preston is no longer allowed here."

"You also said she wouldn't sit in on any meetings but she barged in here anyway. Who's to say she won't show up and wait in her car, to get Raina? In order to keep my daughter protected, she won't be returning." I walked to the door and turned around.

"As far as, Ms. Preston goes. She'll regret ever knowing me or my daughter."

"Mr. Wells."

"What?" I snapped.

"Nothing." She put her head down.

"Oh yea. If you mention this to anyone, I will kill your family." She nodded and grabbed some tissue to wipe her face. I closed the door, grabbed Raina's hand and walked out to go get my mother.

****

"What's up Ryan?" One of the cops spoke when I stepped in the police station.

"What up?" We exchanged man hugs and he led me in the room with my mom. She was sitting there speaking to the same women officers that were here when I picked Khloe up for fighting those damn kids. I still get a kick outta that shit.

"Hey ma." She turned around.

"You again? Does everyone in your family fight? First your girl and now your mom. Is she next?" She pointed to Raina and I gave her a fake smile.

"What the fuck ever. You ready?" My mom stood and told the ladies goodbye, while I gave both of them the finger. Yea, petty as hell but who cares. I handed her the keys and told both of them to wait for me outside.

"This way Ryan." The cop already knew what was up and asked no questions. He opened the cell and left me alone. This stupid bitch had the nerve to grin when she saw me. I leaned against the bars and stared at her. In another life, Sandy may have been a good woman but not in this one.

"Ryan. I'm glad you're here. We need to talk about Raina."

"Oh yea. What about?" I wiped some lint off my jeans and listened to her speak about the incident at the office. Of course, leaving her involvement out of it.

"Sandy, did you put your hands on my daughter?" I lifted my leg and waited for her to answer.

"Absolutely not!" I laughed as she denied it.

"Well, your colleague disagrees and so does your boss and the officers who informed me of you smacking Raina."

"Ryan., I would never lay hands on Raina. She's been through so much." Sandy brought up the fact Khloe attacked her at some doctor's office, which I know isn't true because K isn't like that. I heard about the shit at the club with the bartender because she called me and now this. I nodded and took in each lie she started speaking.

"Sandy you were a good therapist, counselor or whatever you call yourself but you got caught up loving a man who didn't reciprocate the same feelings. Therefore, you attacked my fiancé, my child and attempted to attack my mom but she hit you first. What type of woman goes through all that for a man who wants nothing to do with her?"

"You don't mean that Ryan." I pushed off the bars with my foot and walked over to her.

"Sandy you were a great fuck don't get me wrong and can suck a mean dick but my fiancé is way better than you."

"Yea right."

"Oh you don't believe me."

"No because you would've never been with me."

"I was only with you to get my dick wet because my dumb ass hurt her in the beginning. However, she returned the favor and its when we both realized no one could satisfy us, the way we could with each other. We found our way back and now she's about to be my wife and eventually have my kid. So I'm gonna ask you one question before I snap your neck and walk outta here and pretend you never existed."

"Wha… Whatttt…" She appeared nervous and started looking around the jail.

"No one is going to save you." I smiled.

"My daughter has gone through a lot in the short time she's been on this earth and you of all people know that. My question to you is, was my dick really worth all this?" I saw the tears falling down her face.

"Ryan." I stood her up and placed myself behind her.

"Shhhh. Its only gonna take a second."

"Please don't."

SNAP! I let her body hit the floor, removed the belt from her pants, put it around her neck and stepped out the room.

If you're wondering, the room she was in had four cement walls and no cameras. I know how you readers be analyzing shit to find out how things are possible. Watch a few crime shows and you'll see that not every room has cameras. How do you think pigs are allowed to attack criminals?

"Yo, I think your inmate committee suicide." I told the cop at the end of the hall.

"What did she do?"

"Looks like she used a belt around her neck and hung herself."

"Oh well. It's one less bitch on the street." He gave me a pound and continued typing away on his phone. Cops ain't shit and that's exactly why I pay them great money to look the other way.

"Daddy can we get something to eat?" Raina asked the moment I opened the door.

"Yup. Where we going?"

"Anywhere."

"The diner it is." She smiled. My daughter love to eat there, so I have no idea why she didn't just say it.

"Is she with Lamar?" My mom asked referring to Sandy.

"Yup. What you ordering when we get here?"

"Good and I don't know yet." The three of us pulled in the diner and enjoyed each other's company. When I said no one would bother my family and get away with it anymore, I meant it. Now, I had to go get my petty ass fiancé from her ignorant ass mother's house. This is gonna be fun.

Khloe

"Girl, look at this shit." I handed my phone to Luna and showed her what Raina sent me about the Sandy bitch. Once she told me the bitch hit her, I was ready to go straight there but then she said her father was on his way. I'm a hundred percent sure Sandy is no longer breathing if he had anything to do with it.

Yes the two of us were still holed up at my moms and had no plans of leaving anytime soon. It wasn't that I didn't miss Ryan, I was giving him space and tryna make myself see that he isn't who he used to be. I forgave him when he brought me home from the club that night and he's apologized ever since and even proposed. Yet, I still allowed an outsider to make me believe he'd never change. I'm blaming myself this time because once I took him back there should've never been any doubt.

I do feel bad about asking him who the other woman was on his mind. In all actuality, after Lamar revealed he purposely had his sister walk into a danger zone, I should've known it would bring up memories. Shit, every now and then I had some of my own between Marcus and me. It didn't by any means insinuate me wanting him but the memories were there and always will be. It's bound to happen when you've been with someone as long as we both were with our ex's.

"Let me find out Ryan got bitches going crazy over his Swanson." I busted out laughing and it felt like one of my stitches ripped open.

"KHLOEEEEEE!" My mom shouted up the steps with an attitude.

"What?" It felt good responding anyway I wanted. I tried not to be disrespectful because she's still my mom but it just happens now.

"Can you come down here before I go to jail?" I hauled ass down the steps assuming somehow Sandy was there. Don't ask me why I thought that; I just did. When I reached the bottom step there he was standing there with an angry look.

"Get yo shit so we could go home." He said in a demanding and calm voice.

110

"Ryan?"

"I'm not gonna say it again. I'll be in the truck." He turned and looked at me again.

"Don't make me come back in here." I folded my arms and watched him walk out the door.

"Why you standing there?" I looked over at my mom.

"Get yo shit and go home."

"Really?"

"Hell yea really. It's no secret your father and I are still fucking and with you here, he won't bring me no dick so you gots to go."

"Ma, you could've gone over there."

"He won't let me know where he lives, you know that." I laughed because my dad was still being petty about that.

"Plus, all my toys are here and..."

"Oh my God. I'm gonna be sick." I gagged and ran back up the steps. If my parents were using toys, I know good and well I didn't wanna be here to listen.

Luna was lying on the bed watching television. She would've came down stairs with me had her foot been out the cast. I was extremely happy that we were friends again. I really did miss her and vice versa. I ended up informing her about my abortion and shockingly she wasn't upset. She said, it's a good thing I didn't tell her because she would've been gone to the clinic with me and begged me to keep the baby. I guess, it was the right thing to do after all.

"What did she want?" I put my shoes on and started grabbing my things.

"She didn't want anything. Ryan told me I better have my ass in his car in a few minutes and he better not have to come back in." She sat up.

"How he find you? Does he know I'm here too?" She was worried he'd tell Waleed.

"I doubt it. He stayed by the door. I think it was to keep him from smacking my mom. You know those two can't stand one another."

"Duhhhhh. No one likes her mean ass."

"I don't like you either. Please tell me you're taking this immigrant with you." My mom was leaning on the door watching me pack.

"Oh shit. No the fuck you didn't." Luna grabbed her crutch and tossed it at my mother.

"Hell no. Get this trick out my house." My mom tried to run over to the bed. I jumped in the middle and unfortunately, shit went from bad to worse. Ryan came in and assumed my mom was tryna hit me and tossed her ass across the room. She fell into the wall and hit her head.

"WHAT THE FUCK HAPPENED TO YOUR FACE?" He barked and everyone stopped moving. When he came in to get me, my hair was down so he couldn't see but it was clear as day to him now.

"Did she do this?" He yanked my mom up by the hair and dragged her across the floor.

"RYAN NO!"

"Talk shit now bitch." Luna said to my mom and hit her in the stomach with the bottom of the crutch. Well more like jabbed it into her.

"Why she in here yelling and if she didn't do it, then who did?" His face was filled with anger.

"Ryan please let her go and Luna stop taunting her."
She stood over top of my mom pretending she was gonna jab
her in the stomach again. I can't even lie. The shit Luna was
doing had me trying hard as hell to hold in my laugh.

"Ryan. We'll talk at the house. Just let her go." He used
his other hand to lift the bandage down and his entire face
turned up.

"Tell me right now, who did this." He let my mom's
hair go and placed the bandage back on.

"Sandy." He sucked his teeth.

"Lucky for her, she's dead already. But you old lady.
Keep my fiancé hidden away from me again and watch what
happens."

"Ryan, she didn't keep me here. I stayed on my own."

"Who cares? She should've called me. The bitch knew
I was looking for you because I hit her up twice asking if she
knew where you were." I snapped my head and looked at my
mom who was holding her stomach.

"Ma, why didn't you tell me he called?"

"You said, you were taking a break." She was still coughing from the crutch hitting her stomach.

"Ok but you still could've told me."

"It don't matter. I would've found your sexy ass anyway." He kissed my lips and I melted.

"And you!" He pointed to Luna.

"Got your husband out here looking all over for you."

"Who cares?" She plopped down on the bed.

"If you don't cut it out. Waleed ain't having no baby by that crazy bitch." He told her and asked where my stuff was.

"How do you know?"

"Because he strapped up every time and before you ask, he brought his own condoms and opened them. She only said it to piss you off and as usual, you fell for it. Let's go Khloe." He took my hand in his.

"You better be happy my girl still loves you because I'd put your ass in the ground with everyone else who did her wrong." He said to my mother as he stepped over her.

"But you ain't in the ground and you did her wrong." Why couldn't my mother keep her mouth shut?

"Then she wouldn't be able to fuck the shit outta me. A nigga ain't killing her and missing out on it." He chucked up the peace sign to her and led the way out.

"Wait! How is Luna going to get home? I can't leave those two here alone." The moment my feet hit the bottom step, guess who was strolling in with a blunt in his mouth? Yup. Her damn ignorant ass husband.

"Your friend better pray I take it easy on her pussy tonight."

"Really Waleed?"

"Hell yea. She had a nigga stressing and jerking himself off. Ain't no way she getting away with that." I couldn't help but laugh.

"What if she doesn't want to?"

"I will never rape my wife but there's are no, "*not tonight's*" with me and she knows it."

"I can't with you."

"Nobody can. I'll hit you up tomorrow Risky. I'm sure she's about to learn a lesson on disappearing too."

"No doubt." They gave one another a pound and he ran up the steps to get Luna. As bad as I wanted to warn her, Ryan gave me the look to mind my business.

"Here." He passed me a tray of food when we sat in the car.

"What's this?"

"Food. Raina wanted to make sure you ate." I opened it up.

"Ryan this is a lot of food. I'm gonna be full."

"Exactly! Because after you eat I'm about to fill you up with all this dick." I smacked him on the arm.

"What? I am." I shook my head laughing at him and started eating. I still had to tell him about the baby but until then, I'm gonna enjoy this good ass food and dick. Lord knows I missed it.

****

"I see we meet again." Some woman said and snapped her fingers in front of me. Two other chicks came over.

"Do I know you?" The woman staring in my face was unfamiliar but evidently, she knew me.

117

"You tryna be funny?"

"Actually, I'm not. I don't have any idea who you are."
I put my head down to fill out the paper at the LabCorp. The
doctor called and said my blood work had to be done. They
needed to check my glucose and other things.

"Aren't you the bitch who had my cousin killed?" I
looked up.

"First off... don't call me a bitch. Second... who is your
cousin and why would I have her killed?"

"Let's go Ashley. Why you fucking with her? You
know if Risky finds out, you're next." The woman tried to pull
her away but she was struggling.

"Nah, fuck this fat bitch. She thinks because she
fucking Risky shit is good."

"What is it you want, Ashley is it?" I placed the
clipboard next to me.

"I wanna know where my cousin is."

"Didn't you just say I had her killed?" I guess she
forgot what she said. How you say I killed her and then wanna
know where she is?

118

"Did you?"

"No because I have no clue who she is."

"Veronica bitch."

"Veronica?" I questioned still tryna remember who this woman is.

"Have you looked for her? Called her phone? Went by her house?"

"Obviously, if I can't find her."

"Maybe she ran away." The nurse called my name to go in the back. I stood next to her.

"Really? Ran away?" She asked with her arms folded and the same snarl on her face.

"Oh now I remember you." I looked her up and down.

"You're the one my friend Luna put to sleep outside the kids' school.

"What?" One of the women asked and you could see how embarrassed the Ashley chick was. Its exactly what she gets for tryna approach me over some bullshit.

"Fuck this bitch." Ashley said and waved me off before they went to leave.

"Oh Ashley. Do you want me to send Luna to see you for a reminder?" I blew her a kiss and followed the nurse. She was mad as hell and I don't care. I'm over all these dumb bitches trying me.

Waleed

"Come here Luna." She rolled her eyes but stood up. Ever since I picked her up from Khloe's mother house she tried to give me the silent treatment. Well, that was after I tore her pussy up for leaving me in the first place.

"I'm not in the mood." She stood in front of me and I kissed her stomach. She was now eight months and my son was taking over in her belly. The doctor said he's six pounds and may be bigger when she delivers.

"She's not having my baby."

"How you know? You slept with her a bunch of times because you were mad. I can't believe..." I stood and pressed my lips on hers.

"Regardless if she were an ex or not, I would never give her my kids. I strapped up and brought the condoms. Luna, I promise you she's not having my kid."

"Waleed, I refuse to stay married.-"

"Shut that shit up." I lifted the shirt over her head and unsnapped the bra.

"No other woman is having my child." I placed kisses on her neck, and caressed both of her breasts.

"You are my only wife." I kissed her lips.

"My only baby mama." I moved down to suck on her titties.

"And the only woman to fuck me good." She sucked her teeth.

"You are." I removed the rest of her clothes and stared. In my eyes she was perfect and no one is gonna come between us again.

"Waleed, if that's your baby?"

"I told you it's not, now lift that one leg on the bed, I'm hungry." For someone who wanted to leave me, she sure as hell did it.

****

"What the fuck you want Dora?" I asked when I picked my phone up. Ever since I put her up she's been nagging the fuck outta me. My own wife don't even bother me like this bitch.

"You're looking sexy." I turned around in the soul food place and there she was sitting at a table. I hung the phone up and placed the order for my food. I didn't notice her because my head was down looking at pictures of the baby Jordan's Luna sent me.

As usual, she was at the mall with Khloe and Raina. Risky and I both had people watching them and made it very clear that if anything happened to them, they would suffer dying consequences.

"Hmph. I see your wife is marking her territory." She pushed her finger in my neck and I smacked it away.

"My wife don't need to mark up shit because she has papers on me. This dick you sweating belongs to her." I grabbed it and her nasty ass licked her lips.

"There's no chance in hell, you'll ever see this dick again."

"Why not Wale? I won't tell, if you don't."

"First off, you're pregnant. Second, why would I risk hurting my wife for a piece of pussy anyone could have?" She sucked her teeth.

"Wale, I love you and…" She started with the fake tears again.

"Bye Dora."

"WALEED, WHY ARE YOU HURTING ME? AFTER THE RAPE, I STAYED WITH YOU AND EVEN AFTER THE THREE ABORTIONS YOU MADE ME GET, I NEVER LEFT. NOW YOU'RE CHEATING ON ME WITH A FAT BITCH. HOW COULD YOU?" This bitch screamed out and everyone started looking at me.

"Dora, I swear to God if you don't stop this bullshit."

"YOU'RE GONNA WHAT? BEAT MY ASS AND PUT ME IN THE HOSPITAL AGAIN? WHAT AM I DOING WRONG WALE?" She was being overdramatic and if I could wring her neck, I would.

"Sir, here's your food and if I were you, I'd stay far away from her."

"I have no idea why she's doing that?"

124

"You better get it under control before your wife finds out." She winked and handed me my change. The owner knew Luna very well and I had no doubt she'd tell her the next time they seen each other.

"WALEED!" Dora shouted and ran out the store behind me. It took all my strength not to pull my gun out on her.

"Yo, get the fuck away from me."

"I need a ride home." This bitch sat on the passenger side and locked the door. I got in and backslapped the fuck outta her.

"Don't ever do no stupid shit like that again."

"Ok damn. I was only playing."

"Those people didn't know you were playing. Tha fuck is wrong with you?" I pulled into traffic and felt her hands on my jeans.

"Dora, I swear if you don't stop."

"Oh stop. Let me just suck it." She kept fucking with my jeans. My one hand was moving her hand away, while I tried to keep my other one on the steering wheel. I couldn't pull over because it was so much traffic, I had no room.

"There you are baby." She said, spit a little and put my dick in her mouth.

"Yooooo."

BOOM! I slammed head first into the back of a big ass truck. I felt the blood leaking down my face and looked over at this stupid bitch. She was grinning with a gash on the side of her head.

"Are you ok sir?" Some woman asked.

"Oh my." She looked down and my dick was still out my jeans. I put it in, zipped my jeans and tried to strangle Dora. I heard someone asking me to step out the car. When I did, my ass hit the ground hard as hell.

Luna

We were at the mall shopping when Waleed's mom called and said the cops came to her house and said he was in an accident. They couldn't get in his phone, so they went to the address on his license. I have no idea why he still had his moms on it but who knows what goes on in his head? Khloe drove because my head was all over the place with bad thoughts. If I got behind the wheel, it ain't no telling if we'd be in rooms next to him.

"Excuse me. My husband was brought in not too long ago by the ambulance." I said to the secretary at the reception desk.

"Ok. What's his name?" I gave her his information and she told me what room he was in. Khloe and Raina were right behind me.

I went to the back and my eyes had to be playing tricks on me because Dirty Dora was standing outside his room, speaking to the doctor. *Did she know he was here?* When the bitch looked at me, something about the smirk on her face told me she was up to no good. Instead of addressing her, I moved past them and went straight in Waleed's room. His mom was sitting next to him and he was asleep. She said he hit someone from behind and hit his head either the window or steering wheel. When he got out the car, he fell on the ground and almost hit it again but someone broke his fall. He had a concussion and some bruising on his face, otherwise he was fine.

"Hello everyone." I turned and Dirty Dora was standing there grinning.

"Why are you here?" I asked and made my way to where she was.

"Oh, I was checking on our man."

"Our man? Am I missing something?"

"Obviously you are. What, you think because he put a baby in you he's faithful?"

"Dora, I'm not about to let you get me upset over your obsession with him. I will ask you to remove yourself from this room before I help you."

"This is a hospital. You have no jurisdiction on who can come here."

"She may not but I know for a fact my boy don't want you here. Especially; starting shit with his wife." Risky said and she backed up.

"Your husband is a good driver; wouldn't you say Luna?"

"Yea he is but what does that have to do with you?"

"Maybe you should ask what he was doing to crash?" She winked and basically skipped her way out.

"What is she talking about Risky?"

"I have no idea. Don't let that bitch get under your skin." He hugged me and we all went back in the room. Khloe and I looked at one another. Dora was tryna tell me something and we both knew it. I wasn't gonna worry about it because what goes on in the dark will surely come out in the light.

After about an hour, the doctor came in and said they were admitting him. They wanted to do a MRI and it was gonna take an hour, plus they needed him to stay for observation. Once he got in the room everyone left and said they'd return in the morning. I asked the nurse for a blanket and sheet to lay on the little couch thing they had. Raina let me keep her iPad to watch movies on Netflix and had the nerve to tell me not to watch any of the movies she had in her que. Talking about those are the parts she had to watch later.

"Hey baby." Waleed said when he opened his eyes.

"How you feeling?" I kissed his lips and he pulled me in close for a deeper one.

"Better now." I ran my hand down his face.

"What happened?" I could see him tense up.

"Man, this guy stopped short and I was tryna open my food from the soul food place. Babe, I wasn't paying attention."

"Hmph."

"Why you say that?"

"Well Dora came to see you, which I found odd because how would she know you were here unless she was with you." He stared but didn't say a word.

"Was she with you Waleed?" It took him a few seconds to respond.

"Nah. Why would she be with me? You know I don't fuck with her like that."

"Then why was she here?"

"Maybe someone else was here she knew." I continued staring, which made him uncomfortable. He was guilty of something. I saw it all over his face and it was killing him to hold it in. However, I know he won't ever incriminate himself either so whatever went down, he's gonna deal with on his own. He better hope he's not cheating because I promise you, a bitch will shoot his fucking dick off.

****

"Push Luna." Waleed yelled as he held my hand in the delivery room. A week after he had the car accident, my water broke and now I'm tryna push my big head son out. He was yelling on one side, while my mom was on the other doing the same thing. My father was in the waiting room because he refused to see me going through pain. I told him they gave me an epidural but he wasn't having it.

"I am pushing asshole. Why don't you reach in there and take him out? Its your fault its taking so long."

131

"How is it my fault?"

"Because he has your big ass head and it probably can't fit." I saw the doctor and nurse laugh.

"I wonder if his dick will be big too. You know to drive the ho's crazy." My mother could no longer contain her laugh and was bent over holding her stomach.

"Ughhhhhh. God why did you send me an asshole husband?"

"Says the woman who loves fucking me." He whispered in my ear and I sucked my teeth.

"There's the head." Waleed let my hand go and went to the end of the bed to record.

"Yo Luna. Your pussy opening up real wide. GOT DAMN!"

"GET OUT!"

"Hell no. Hurry up and push so I can hold my son." I gave one more push and it felt as if my insides came gushing out. I heard my son screaming and laid back on the bed. The doctor handed him to the nurse and told me to push the afterbirth out. I felt so relieved down there.

132

"Damn, he's tiny." I lifted my head and Waleed was standing next to the nurse as she weighed and washed him off. Usually they place him on the mothers' chest but I told them, I didn't want blood all over me. Yea, it's mine but it's still nasty. Plus, I knew I'd be tired and ready to fall asleep like I am now. Once the doctor sewed me up, my eyes closed and a bitch was in la la land.

I woke up and Waleed was on the chair with our son lying on his chest. He was asleep too but you could tell he had a firm grip on him. I reached over for my phone and snapped a photo. My husband may be an asshole, ignorant and get on my nerves but he's mime and I'm not going to let another bitch come destroy our happiness. When I heal, I'm gonna make it my business to see Dora and if shit ain't right, its gonna be hell to pay.

Risky

"Ryan we need to talk." Khloe said when she stepped in the house. Hell yea, she's been here since I went and got her. She's my fiancé now so it ain't no leaving me.

"What up?" I shut the television off to give her my undivided attention. You could see how nervous she was because her face was flustered. I went to where she stood and tears started falling down her face.

"What's wrong?"

"Why doesn't anyone want me to be happy?" I had no idea what she was talking about. Her and Luna were on speaking terms again. Sandy and Veronica were gone and as far as I knew, she had no enemies.

"I'm lost. Who don't want you to be happy?"

"It seems like everyone is against me." She moved in the living room and started pacing back and forth. Raina strolled in and asked what was wrong too.

"Veronica hated me, Sandy tried to kill me." She pointed to her face that she just had the stitches taken out of. I still get pissed when I see the scar. I promised to take her to see a plastic surgeon to fix it whenever she's ready.

"Then, I go to LabCorp to get blood work done and Ashley approaches me, and says I think I'm better than everyone because I have you." She went there weeks ago, so why is she bringing this up now? She never told me anyone bothered her and why is Ashley even saying shit to her in the first place?

"Ugh, I hate to break it to you but you are." I shrugged my shoulders. Raina and Khloe both sucked their teeth.

"Ryan, I'm not supposed to be pregnant and stressed out. It's not good for the baby and..."

"Whoa. Whoa. Whoa. What did you just say?" She stopped pacing and thank God because that shit was driving me crazy.

"Oh, I'm pregnant and..."

"YOU ARE!" Raina and I both shouted at the same time.

"Yes but Ryan you're not listening." She was still tryna tell me some bullshit story about people not liking her. All I cared about was her announcing she's pregnant.

"Damn, I love you." I said and slid my tongue in her mouth.

"Really dad? Ugh, y'all make me sick." She tried to walk out the room.

"Awwww, I love you too Raina. Give your dad a big hug." I scooped her up and she was screaming for me to let her go.

"Ryan, put her down."

"Thanks mommy." It was like time stood still when Raina called her that. I was stuck and so was Khloe.

"What? I can't call you that?" I could tell Khloe was tryna think of the right words, where I was surprised she even wanted to call her that. It took both of us a minute to answer.

"Ummm." Khloe was still stuck. I had to tell her to speak.

"Raina, I would never try and take your moms place." I could see my daughter looking confused.

"I know. I called you that because Ms. K sounds like a teacher name and I shouldn't call you by your real name if you're gonna be my mom." Its obvious Raina already thought about this.

"Ugh. Ok."

"Look Ms. K, if you don't want me to call you mommy, I won't. But you are the closest person to my dad that I've even consider calling mom. Yes, he was with that other woman but she was never mother material."

"Are you sure that's what you want?" I asked and could tell Khloe was thinking the same thing.

"Absolutely and you know why?

"Why?" We both asked at the same time. Hell, I was curious myself.

"Because you couldn't stand me when we first met and yet; you've been the glue that held me and my dad together. To be honest, you're the one who got me to open up and be comfortable in my own skin."

"Raina."

"You are and even though my dad probably said it a thousand times, thank you for being there even when it was rough. I know, I'm a hard person to get along with but you saw right through me. When you and my dad weren't speaking, you still stayed by my side."

"Of course."

"Thank you for loving my dad and showing him what real love is, after my mom. And thank you for loving and protecting me as your own." I smiled because at times when Khloe hated me, she never neglected Raina.

"I love you Ms. K and I'm glad my father picked you to be his wife, the mother of my brother or sister and my mom." Khloe was hysterical crying and Raina went over to hug her. It took her a few minutes to get it together.

"I love you too Raina. You can call me mom but I want you to know that I'm not trying to take her spot. I will continue teaching you how to be a woman and anything else you need."

"Can you do me a favor though?" Raina asked Khloe who was wiping her eyes.

"What is it?"

138

"Can you tell your friend to stop calling my phone?"

"What happened?"

"Nothing really and I don't mind relaying messages but when her and uncle Waleed aren't speaking, why she always yelling at me?" We busted out laughing. When Luna couldn't reach Khloe, she would call my daughter and vent a little to her. She wouldn't tell her too much but enough to get on Raina's nerves.

"I'm gonna talk to her about that. She shouldn't be telling my daughter anything." Raina smiled and went upstairs to her room. I could tell she was happy about Raina calling her mommy.

"How far are you?" I rubbed her stomach.

"I'm almost three months."

"When was the doctor's appointment?" I asked with my hand still on her belly. I couldn't believe we were finally about to have a kid.

"The last one was the day after Waleed had the accident. You were stressed out and I didn't want to bother you."

"That wouldn't have bothered me."

139

"I'm sorry for not telling you. The next one is in two weeks and I want you to come. She's gonna attempt to tell us what we're having."

"Oh yea?"

"Yea. I told her I'll only find out if you're with me. Plus, I want you to see the baby on the screen in 3D. Its totally different then the photo." She was overjoyed and its all I ever wanted for her. If I have to plant a kid in her ever year to see her this happy, then I'll do it.

"Are you happy?"

"I am but I'm scared. What if?-" I stopped her before she could finish.

"You're gonna be fine."

"But..."

"I'm gonna handle Ashley and anyone else who bothers you. No one is going to make you lose my kid." She nodded.

"Baby, I don't want you to get in trouble."

"Never." I placed a kiss on her lips and stood her up.

Khloe is definitely the woman I'm supposed to marry. Don't get me wrong, I loved the hell outta Lacey and she would've been my wife too but I can't help but feel, that her dying was God's way of putting Khloe in my life. Everything about her is perfect and I don't see myself without her.

"I'm gonna order dinner so go upstairs, take a hot bath and relax. Your man got you."

"I'm sorry for listening to outsiders and staying with my mother, who by the way hates you even more now." I laughed because her father called me and said she told him what happened. The crazy part is, he asked if anyone recorded it. He loved her but he said she's getting everything she deserved for being mean to Khloe all those years and I couldn't agree more.

"It's in the past and your mother knows I don't care. The only woman I care about hating me, is you and I'm not letting it happen."

"Good because I have a surprise for you after Raina goes to bed."

"Oh yea." She bit down on her lip.

"Yup and I'm positive you're gonna like it."

"Let me give her some Benadryl so she can go to sleep early." I thought she was gonna fall from laughing so hard.

"What?"

"Benadryl Ryan?"

"Why not? It makes you go to sleep and if my surprise is what I think it is, she needs to be knocked out ASAP."

She shook her head and when she made it upstairs, told me I better not give it to her. I may not give it to Raina but after dinner, I'm locking the house down and going in the bedroom to get my surprise. Early or not, she's gonna give it to me.

****

"About time bro." Waleed said and gave me a pound.

"Man, she should've been pregnant but her ass had to be taking those damn pills. Ain't no way, Luna's ass should've had your son already when K and I hooked up first."

"True but she hated you. Why give a nigga a kid when the father was being a jerk?"

"I learned my damn lesson though."

"What's that?" He asked.

142

"No matter what a woman looks like on the outside, it's what's on the inside that counts."

"If you don't stop tryna sound like ma dukes."

"Nigga, I got that off TV." We fell out laughing. It was true. Raina and I were watching some show and a woman told her daughter that. It made sense so of course I used it.

"Risky can you tell me where my cousin is?" I turned around to see Ashley standing there with her hands on her hip. I yoked her stupid ass up.

"If you approach my fiancé again with your bullshit, I promise you'll see Veronica sooner than later. Think I'm playing if you want." I pushed her so hard, she fell into the wall. I never answered her questioned and dared her to ask again.

"I keep telling these bitches to leave Khloe alone." The bartender said.

"They'll learn one day and thanks again for having her back when dumb ass Sandy was in here."

"You know I got you." She winked and went to help other customers.

I stared at her ass and reminisced for a few seconds. Yea we used to fuck around before Veronica but we both had a lot going on. Lacey passed away a year before and she had just broken up with her man. We were there to satisfy each other's needs at the time, yet; stayed friends afterwards.

"Where you going?" I asked Waleed who stood up.

"If I told you, you wouldn't believe me." He gave me a pound and said he'd speak to me tomorrow. When he got like this, something was up. He'll tell me when he's ready. Until then, I'm going home and handle my woman who's been sending me nasty text messages. All I know is, she better be ready when I get there.

Waleed

"What are you doing husband?" I hated when she called me that. She only did it when I pissed her off or did something she didn't like.

"Changing my son. What it look like, wife?"

"Waleed, why you got him butt naked though? All you had to do was take his pants down, unbutton the onesie and change him." I looked down and it did look crazy.

"How in the hell am I supposed to know that?" She busted out laughing and moved me out the way.

"Whatever." I paid attention and she was done changing him in no time.

"Ok, now give him back." She had him on her shoulder.

"Waleed, you had him all day. Don't you have somewhere to go?" I sucked my teeth, kissed my son on his forehead and her on the lips.

"Mmmmmm. Don't leave daddy." She bit her lip and my dick bricked right up.

"Stop playing Luna." Its been three weeks since she had my son and both of us were adamant about not having another kid until the shit with Oscar and Julie is over.

"Wait right here." She left me standing in the room and closed the door. I lifted my phone off the clip and received a text from Dora. This bitch is testing the hell outta me.

I opened it and she was playing in her pussy. I frowned my face because not only was she trifling, it didn't even look sexy. My wife played with her titties better than she did her pussy. I sent her a message back telling her she's blocked and not to call or text me from any other numbers.

I don't know why I didn't leave that bitch homeless. I told her to get the fuck out the house and she told me, if I came around and made her leave she'd tell Luna about the accident. The fact she was able to hold something over my head only pissed me off more and eventually, I'm gonna kill her. She thinks everything is funny. I got a trick for ass though.

"What's wrong?" Luna asked, closed the door and locked it.

"Where's my son?"

"Downstairs with your mom." I forgot she was here.

"Let your wife take care of you." She removed her top and turned some music on. I can't even tell you what song was on because she was doing a strip show for me. Yea, we were waiting to have sex but her period was off so her standing her naked had me stuck. I wanted her real bad and she must've felt the same.

"I miss you inside me baby." She took my finger and placed it in her mouth and put my other hand on her pussy. She was already dripping wet.

"Luna, you know I'm not gonna pull out." I stood up and allowed her to take my clothes off. That shit was sexy as hell to me.

"You will because I'm gonna suck all those babies out just the way you like it."

"Got damn you sexy as fuck." She pushed me on the bed, climbed on top and slid down.

"Arghhhh." She moaned out in pain and I hated to see her like that.

"Its ok babe. I have to get used to you again." She rocked back and forth slow, then sped up and started doing her thing. My finger was caressing her clit and the harder she became, the faster she rode me.

"Cum for your husband Luna." I circled faster and our tongues were dancing together.

"Yea ma. You look so damn good cumming for me." Her body was still shaking.

I flipped her over, lifted those legs on my shoulder and pummeled the hell outta her pussy. When you're used to getting it a lot and it stops for whatever reason, you enjoy every moment as if its your last. Every facial expression she made and every moan that escaped her lips only heightened the experience we were both encountering at the moment. As I stared into her eyes, all I saw was love and I'm sure she could see the same in mine.

"I'm sorry Luna, but I'm about to cum." She lifted my chest to tell me to move, pushed me back and literally sucked every single baby I had out. I yanked her up by the hair and threw my tongue down her throat.

"I love you Luna and know I'm gonna find that nigga and your sister." She wrapped her arms around my neck.

"I love you too and I have no doubt you'll do whatever it takes to keep us safe." And just like that we were at it again. All I know is my ass didn't leave the house at all.

****

"I'm gonna have to kill Dora." I told Risky as we sat in the funeral home waiting on Luna's pop to show up.

"Man, you know damn well she would be a problem. What were you thinking allowing her in your whip?"

"Bro, she jumped her dirty ass in, locked the door and wouldn't get out. Ain't nobody got time to play those games with her. I figured if I took her home she'd be fine. Who the hell knew she'd put my dick in her mouth?" He raised his eyebrows.

"You're right. I should've known better but damn."

"Look. Maybe you should go ahead and tell Luna. That way Dora has nothing over your head."

"Are you crazy? Luna will literally shoot my ass." He thought shit was hilarious, where my ass is nervous.

149

"Hello gentlemen." We turned around and my father in law was standing there smoking a cigar. We both spoke and waited for him to get comfortable in his seat. He passed me an envelope and told me to open it.

I lifted the flap and glanced over the papers. It was Julie's medical records, which I'm not sure why he gave them to me. It had her blood type on it along with the abortion she had some years back and a few other things. What really caught my attention is the fact her son may not be Oscar's. There was some paper asking for a paternity test from a man who remained anonymous.

"OH SHITTTTTTT! Is this what I think it is?"

"Yup. I figured Luna didn't give you these papers a while ago when I gave them to her."

"Nah, she didn't." I looked on the paper again and noticed it was petitioned not too long ago.

"Yooooooo Oscar is gonna have a fit."

"Exactly! Which is why I told my hard headed daughter to give you these sooner. You could've used this ammunition the day he had my daughter at the mall."

"How the hell did they get away with this?" He smirked and at first, I thought it was a made up document until he told me otherwise.

"When Oscar met my daughter in Mexico, I knew all about it." I was shocked to hear him say that.

"I promised my wife that I wouldn't kill her so I left her alone. She ended up making Oscar fall in love, which made me happy because it meant he would stop harassing Luna."

"Say what?" He proceeded to inform me of how Oscar loved Luna and how hurt he was when she left him alone for trying to get her pregnant; per his father."

"Damn."

"Anyway, he fell hard for Julie but his cheating kept getting him in trouble. She left him, moved back here and that's when she met you. You two were hot and heavy, Oscar found out about the child, made her terminate it and come home. Supposedly they were on good terms since then. Now here's where the plot thickens." I sat the papers on the desk and prepared myself for what he would say next. Risky sat there just as surprised.

"Oscar went away on week long vacations many times and each time his father would find his way to their house. He claimed it was to check on her but evidently, the two of them were sleeping together. Don't ask me why she wanted an older man but his purpose was strictly to get the empire."

"What?" I said.

"If Oscar married Luna, he's get the empire. His father was gonna have Oscar leave it to him in his will. Afterwards, Oscar and Julie would suffer a fatal accident, in which he would have control of everything; including my grandkids."

"No shit."

"So you see, Oscar could care less about the empire. It's Julie who wanted it just to hurt Luna and his father wants it because he's a greedy bastard."

"But Luna could care less about it." I told him. She wanted nothing to do with it.

"Yea but they don't know that. They're under the assumption, you and her got married to keep it from them." I gave him the side eye.

"True or not, all the years of hard work was not going down the drain because Oscar's father is on some hunt to run the world." He stood up to leave.

"Hold up. Why don't you want him to have any parts of it? I thought he was your partner in the beginning."

"He was until he got behind those bars and sung like a canary."

"Get the fuck outta here. Ain't no way he snitched." I said.

"You have no idea what people will do for lesser time."

"Damn that's crazy." Risky was shaking his head.

"Luckily, I know a lotta people so everyone he sung his heart out to, no longer walk this earth." He opened the door and turned around.

"Oh yea. You better tell my daughter about that Dora bitch because I can see her shooting your pecker off."

"How the hell did you know?"

"It's my job to know anything concerning my daughter and son in law." He winked.

"Hold up." I ran behind him.

"I don't know how to tell her. The shit was an accident. She jumped in my car for a ride and.-" He cut me off.

"Tell her the truth. Tell her the bitch is crazy, and that you tried to keep her from behind by homeless but she took advantage. Trust me, she'll respect you more for telling her before someone else does." I nodded and he left me standing there with something to think about. Should I tell her? Hell yea because Dora was definitely gonna show her ass.

Khloe

"Thanks for coming with me." I said to Luna who wanted to get out the house. Waleed was meeting with Ryan at the funeral home and her mom had the baby.

"Its not like I had other shit to do." She closed the door.

We were on our way to collect rent from the rental properties Ryan owned. He kept saying he'd do it but here it is the middle of the month and he hasn't even thought about it. The only reason I'm doing it is because he asked me to make sure his books are up to date. He basically had to beg me because I didn't want to know how much money he had but he said, since I'm going to be his wife who cares? All I can say, is his bank account was lovely and so were the two he had overseas.

I admit when he gave me the stuff from his office, it was a damn mess. Shit was everywhere and whoever he had doing it had no idea what they were doing. No money was missing and it was accounted for but Lord knows he doesn't need an auditor coming in asking questions and he had no answers.

I called most of the tenants and let them know I was coming just in case they had something to do. And if they did, I told them to leave it in the mailbox.

We pulled up to the first house and the woman was standing outside waiting for me. I collected the check, handed the woman a card with an address to a P.O. Box on it and told her from now on to mail her rent check to that address. That way, I don't have to do this every month. She said, ok and went about her business.

The two of us drove to the next two places and I handed each of those tenants a card as well and kept it moving. The last house was a four or five family and rather nice for the neighborhood it was in. It wasn't the hood but it was a lot nicer than the ones around it. We got out, walked up the steps and knocked on each door. The tenants came out but when we made it to the top floor, you could hear music blasting, smell weed and it sounded like a bunch of people. The closer we got the stronger the smell became and it was definitely overwhelming for a pregnant woman. We heard someone suck their teeth and turned around.

"I hope you're here to toss her trifling ass out." One of the tenants we just collected rent from said. I thought she went in her house but obviously not.

"How long has this been going on?"

"About a month or so. It wasn't as bad until recently. Its like she doesn't care that we have kids and work."

"She?" Luna and I yelled out. With the weed smell, I automatically assumed it would be a guy and his friends.

"Yes. The little heffa got cursed out by me quite and a few times, I wanted to go upside her head."

"Did you contact Mr. Wells?" I asked wondering why he hasn't been over here to check this person.

"Yea, he said he'd be here this week to talk to her."

"He's been very busy but I'm gonna try and deal with it now. If not, I'll make sure he comes here when he gets home."

"Thanks love and congratulations." We both looked at her.

"You're expecting right?"

"How did you know?" She smiled.

"You have a glow around you and Mr. Wells told me his fiancé was having a baby."

"Really?"

"Yes and I must say, he's ecstatic." She winked and closed her door.

"Ok bitch. Everyone knows about you."

"They better." I knocked on the door and no one answered. I did it again and the same thing. Luna's crazy ass started kicking it and boy were we surprised by who answered it.

"What the fuck you two fat bitches want?" Ashely said and smirked.

"I'm gonna remain calm at the moment but if you call me out my name again, I promise to slide your ass down these fucking steps. Now first things first. Where is the rent?"

"Rent?" She questioned as if she didn't understand English.

"Yes rent. You know money the landlord gets at the beginning of each month." Luna said, pissing her off.

"Well, I don't live here and it's the middle of the month." She smirked.

"If you don't stay here, then who does?" Ashley opened the door wider and there was Dora standing there with a grin on her face.

There were a few people sitting on the couch and some in the kitchen. I pushed past Ashley and fanned myself as I walked through the place. I have to say, it was laid out and I'm shocked she could afford this type of luxury. Ryan told me she solely depended on Lamar and now that he's gone, she had no one. Her family lives in the projects and she has no bank account so how is she living like this?

"Can I help you two ladies?" Dora asked and came closer to us. I stepped in front of Luna because it seemed like she was about to say some foul shit.

"Is this your apartment?"

"Yes."

"Ok, well I'm here to collect the rent on behalf of my fiancé." I said and turned to look at Ashley who sucked her teeth.

159

"Rent? Tsk." She had the nerve to wave me off. I grabbed her wrist.

"Yes rent. Where is it?"

"Why don't you ask her husband?"

"Why in the hell would he know where your rent is?" Luna stepped around me. The music stopped and everyone was staring in our direction.

"Honey, you really should communicate more with your man. You see..." She stepped m Luna's face.

"He put me in this apartment and has been taking care of me and my child." She rubbed her stomach. My mouth was hanging.

"Whose baby is that?"

"I should tell you his but I'm not that desperate to piss you off. But then again maybe I will."

"If it ain't his baby, how else would you piss me off besides being a dirty bitch tryna live off someone else's man?"

"Oh, he didn't tell you."

"Tell me what?" She smiled and had the nerve to tell everyone to listen to what she was about to say. At that moment, I knew she was about to embarrass the hell outta

Luna. I tried to pull her out the door but she wasn't having it. I

sent a text to Ryan because this is about to get ugly and I can't

guarantee, me and Ashley won't get it popping.

"The day your so-called husband was in the accident,

the two of us met up at the soul food place. I got in the car with

him, undid his jeans and sucked his soul out. Why you think he

crashed, when we all know how good a driver he is?"

"DORA!" Ashley shouted as if she didn't know.

"What? This bitch always talking shit about how

perfect her man is. Well guess what, he ain't as perfect as you

say, now is he?" Hurt was written all over Luna's face and I

think everyone noticed it.

"Well, I guess you got what you wanted."

"Not really. That dick is amazing inside me but he

won't fuck me because of you." Luna nodded, pushed past her

and went into the bedroom. You heard a few things fall and all

of a sudden Luna came out with a handful of clothes. She

dropped them in the hallway and went in the kitchen to grab a garbage bag. No one said a word and the second time she came from the room we figured she was kicking Dora out.

"What the fuck you doing?"

"Bitch, you're moving."

"No I'm not. Your husband said I could live here." Luna laughed and hooked off on Dora so hard, she fell into Ashely. The guys in the apartment started leaving one by one.

"Can you do me a favor and take these bags down please?" Luna asked one of the guys and he did it. She moved closer to Dora.

"Listen here, you sneaky, disgusting, conniving, manipulating bitch." She had her finger in Dora's face.

"I don't give a fuck what my husband told you. He's not taking care of no bitch. If you don't believe me, call him."

"I don't have to do shit. Like I said, I'm not going anywhere."

"That's where you're wrong." Luna grabbed her by the hair and literally drug her down the steps by the weave. I know some of her hair had to be separating from her scalp. The woman who told us about her, opened the door and laughed.

"GET OFF ME." Dora tried to pry Luna's hands off but it wasn't working. By the time we reached the front door, Ryan and Waleed were pulling up. Ryan jumped out and Waleed punk ass stood outside the door and sparked up a blunt.

"Come get your bitch Waleed." He blew smoke in the air and stayed quiet.

"What's going on?" Ryan pulled me to the side. I told him what went down and he just shook his head. I wasn't gonna ask if he knew Dora was there because that's his best friend and it would be stupid of me to assume he'd tell on him.

"BITCH, I'M GONNA FUCK YOU UP." Dora screamed out and attempted to run after Luna.

CLICK! Is all you heard. Waleed had his gun out and the blunt was hanging on the side of his lip.

"You gonna do what to my wife?" Luna stood there with her arms folded and Ashley was shaking her head.

"Waleed, she came in kicking me out and.-"

"And what? She's my wife and if she said you had to go, then get to fucking stepping."

"But you said."

"I tried to be nice to keep you from being homeless. You pull that bullshit in my car, making me crash. Then you had the fucking nerve to start blackmailing me. My wife will always be first in my life, you dumb bitch. What she says, goes. Now beat it."

"I hate you Waleed."

"Join the fucking club." He pushed her down the street. Her and Ashely got in the car and sped off. I'm sure this is not the last time we see them.

"You ok? Ashley didn't touch you, did she?"

"I'm ok and no she didn't touch me. I think my fiancé instilled fear in her, therefore; she knew not to lay hands on me." I wrapped my arms around his neck and placed a soft kiss on his lips.

"Can you hang tonight? Your man needs some of this." He let his hand go in my leggings.

"Baby."

"What? They not paying attention." I took his hand out and put in it my mouth.

"Look at my nasty freak."

"I'll be every freak in the book for you."

"That's exactly why I'm strung out." He said and kissed me. He took my hand and walked me to the truck.

"See you soon."

"You know our daughter is gonna be with your mother tonight, so we get to be real nasty." He grabbed himself.

"I'm about to drop him off. I'll be right there." I started laughing and watched him run to his truck. Luna and Waleed were staring each other down. I was definitely taking her home and anxiously await my future husband. I must say, he was well worth the wait. The two of us are gonna do so many nasty things, we should be arrested for sex crimes.

Luna

When Khloe asked me to accompany her to Risky's appointment to collect the rent, I had no problem. My husband was out, my mom had my son so there wasn't anything else for me to do. We were planning on grabbing dinner afterwards but as luck would have it, this dirty bitch was in one of the apartments claiming my man was financing her stay. Now me being who I am, questioned her and after hearing enough, tossed her and all her shit out. Who did she think she was talking shit to and tryna make me look a fool? I swear, I tried to hold in my anger but she had a way of bringing it out.

Anyway, the people she had in the apartment paid more attention to me kicking her out, then smoking or whatever else they were in there doing. Its crazy because I assumed they would be at least recording shit. This generation coming up relied on social media on a daily basis. I guess they weren't beat, especially after hearing who my man was. I can't say any of them worked with him but I will say, his name and kill game is well known in the streets. Hell, even I know that.

After kicking her out and running into Waleed outside, the two of us gave one another a stare down but neither of us spoke. I'm sure he was tryna figure out what to say, where I wanted to murder him. I looked at Khloe and hated to see how in love she and Risky were. Don't get me wrong, I'm still in love with my husband but he had more baggage then a little bit with his ex's. At least, Oscar don't bother me this much. Granted, he wants to kill is but he's staying away for the time being.

"I'm staying with y'all tonight." She snapped her neck when I said it as I closed the door.

"Luna, you know I love you and would never push you off but my fiancé wants to be extra nasty tonight so if you don't have a problem listening to a porn movie, be my guest." I looked at her and rolled my eyes.

"Never mind. Take me to my mothers. I refused to listen to you nasty fuckers."

"You gonna be ok?" She asked and drove off.

"Yea. I'm sure he had all types of excuses on why he did this or why he did that but I'm not tryna hear shit right now. Say what you want but he's receiving the silent treatment until I'm ready to talk."

"I understand. I'd probably be doing the same thing to Ryan."

"I love you boo." She dropped me off at my moms and sped out the driveway. I went inside to soak in my own tears.

****

This nigga had me all the way fucked up. Its been two days since the shit at the apartment and I haven't spoken to Waleed. Yes, he called me constantly but I refused to answer. I'm sure my mom told him where I was because he didn't threaten me about my whereabouts.

How the hell was he taking care of his ex when he has a wife and son? Granted, I wasn't screwing him every other day because its only been a short time since I delivered and we both agreed to wait on having more kids. I wonder if he had sex with her? And what did she mean, her sucking his dick is the reason he crashed? That's definitely not the way he told me the accident happened.

I paced around this room for fucking hours tryna calm myself down. Tryna calm the thoughts running rampant in my head down. Tryna figure out if what Dora said is true because I never asked him and he had no problem tossing her out. Then again, he did say she did some foul stuff and blackmailed him. I ran down the steps at my parents, grabbed some car keys since my car was home and drove to my house.

I got there in record time, hit the alarm on the car, used my key to get in and stormed up the steps. Music was playing in the room and it smelled like incense were burning. I know damn well this motherfucker wasn't bold enough to bring no bitch in this house.

I opened the door and he was sitting there in just a towel with water still clinging to his skin. Candles were lit and he had some I Love You balloons in the corner. I noticed two black velvet boxes on the dresser as well and a few bags from Gucci. Lately, I've become infatuated with that store for some reason. Was he waiting for me? Did he know I was coming? I bet my mother called with her nosy ass. She loved Waleed so of course, she'd tell him.

"I'm sorry." He said and kept his head looking at the ground.

"Did I do something wrong?" Was my first question. He didn't say anything which instantly put me on defense.

"Is it because you were horny? Why would you let her touch you?" He looked at me and I instantly broke down. How could my husband allow another woman to touch him? He came over to me and placed his hands on my face.

"You did nothing wrong and I'll stay horny for months if I had to and I didn't let her touch me."

"Then how did all of this happen?" I wiped my eyes and he had me take a seat on the bed.

"She asked for a ride, well jumped in my car and wouldn't get out. I drove off and she kept tryna get my pants unbuttoned." I sucked my teeth because even though I asked the questions, I'm not sure I wanted to know.

"Luna, I tried to pull over to stop her but it was so much traffic, I couldn't. It literally only happened for maybe two seconds because I crashed."

"Waleed."

"I tried to strangle her afterwards but I passed out. Luna, I would never intentionally hurt you and I hope you know that." He kissed me passionately and I smacked fire from his ass. The look on his face was scary but I know he wouldn't hurt me. My fists started connecting with his chest and a few times in his face. Once I was tired, he snatched me up, stripped me out my clothes and fucked me straight to sleep.

****

"That's twice you put your hands on me. I can't promise that if it happens again I won't react." He said the next morning when he brought me breakfast in bed.

"I'm sorry Waleed. I should've never hit you, especially; when you don't hit me. I get so angry and it's the only way to make you feel my pain."

"I know and from here on out, I promise to do better." He lifted my face to stare at him.

171

"I'm no woman beater but I need you to really understand that I don't play that hitting on me shit. Wife or not, I'll leave you." He was sincere and the tone of his voice told me never to lay hands on him again. I had to figure out a way to change the subject so he doesn't have a flashback and leave me.

"Do you want to sleep with her? Is that why you gave her somewhere to stay?"

"I'm not gonna lie and say she hadn't offered herself to me because she did. But there's no way in hell, I'd ever hurt you like that."

"But you did."

"I was gonna tell you after the meeting with your pops but Khloe text Risky that things were getting outta hand at the apartment. When he told me which one you were at, I knew Dora told you. I should've told you sooner but you were pregnant with my son and I wasn't about to stress you out." I nodded and continued eating.

"Oh. By the way, you're most likely pregnant again." I sucked my teeth. He refused to pull out last night and I know it was on purpose, which is why I didn't even fight him on it.

"I'm glad it's out because she definitely tried to use it to her advantage." He said and started telling me all the nasty messages she sent him and said if he didn't do certain things she'd tell. It was really pathetic to hear the lengths she went through for his attention.

"Hurry up and get dressed. I wanna go see Black Panther before we pick my son up." I sucked my teeth.

"Waleed that movie is long. Why do we have to go?" I whined.

"Same reason why I had to eat that pussy more than once last night."

"You had some making up to do so don't give me that."

"You got that. Hurry up." He left me in the room eating the rest of my breakfast. I knew Dora was at the hospital the day of the accident for a reason. I hate she held it over his head but its nothing like making sure she gets what she deserves, which I will do soon.

Julie

"Gerald, what do you want me to do? You're threatening my kids." I said to Oscars father who was on the phone asking why his son changed his mind on wanting the empire.

"Julie, that is my shit so you better get on board with making him want it."

"Gerald, don't you think it's time to let this go? For the sake of your son, your grandkids and wife."

"First off bitch, those may be my kids." I cringed when he said that. Before anyone judges me, let me explain.

A few years ago, Oscar went away about once or twice a month for business. His father would come by to check on me and make sure I didn't need anything. I never thought twice about allowing him in because that's his father. He'd take me to the store if needed and other places as well.

Anyway, one night he stopped by drunk as hell. I tried to take him home in my own vehicle but once he hit the couch he refused to get up. Instead of fighting with him, I grabbed a blanket, covered him up and went to bed. Oscar was coming home the following night and I planned on telling him about his father's behavior.

That same night, I felt my legs being lifted and a mouth on my pussy. Now I'm thinking Oscar came home to surprise me but little did I know; his father had snuck in the room. I didn't realize it was him until he made me cum a few times, climbed in top and I smelled the alcohol. It was coming though his pores and mixed in with his morning breath. People may not care for me but trust me when I say, I tried my hardest to push him off.

Long story short, he continued raping me until he came. When he got up, I laid there crying my eyes out because I had no idea what to do. Would Oscar believe me? Would he kill me? There were so many thoughts in my head I was going crazy. Unfortunately, I popped up pregnant but I was a hundred percent sure it was Oscar's because of the time frame. I was three months and he attacked me the previous month.

However, after delivering my daughter, Oscar started to go away again. I begged to go with him and he had no idea why. I wanted to tell him but was scared. He left anyway and once again his father continued to rape me. (*No, I didn't allow him in the house*.) He had a key and when I had the locks changed, Oscar gave him the new one. I was lost and alone. My mother was dead, my sister hated me and my father wanted my head. The only person who helped me was my stepmother. Yes, I said it. My stepmother.

"Hello."

"Mommy, I need help." I called her that ever since she accepted me as her own child.

"Julie? Oh my God. Where have you been? Are you ok? I missed you so much." She bombarded me with questions and I could hear her sniffling.

"Mommy, he won't leave me alone."

"Who honey? Who won't leave you alone?"

"Gerald. Oscar's father. He keeps raping me and now I'm pregnant. I don't know if it's his or Oscar's. He's gonna kill me."

"Where are you?"

"I'm scared to tell you."

"I can't help you, if you don't tell me." I gave her the address.

"I'll be on the first flight out." I hung up and prayed she'd be here before Gerald returned. Oscar was due to leave tomorrow and I know his father would come right after.

The following day, my stepmother arrived and when I say she was bad, she really was. I couldn't believe she came to help me especially after I almost killed her. After hugging and crying, she had me tell her in detail what was going on. She hopped on the phone and started speaking a different language to someone. Twenty minutes later, about four men arrived and told me they were waiting for Gerald. What a lot of people don't realize is, my father may run the cartel but my stepmother has her own connections.

That night around eleven, Gerald pulled in my driveway. She had me taken daughter upstairs and said not to come out the room. Of course, I did anyway because my nosy ass wanted to see her handle him. Imagine my surprise when he saw her and pretended to hug him. She stuck some needle in his neck that put him on his knees. The men immediately starting whooping his ass.

"If you ever come near my daughter again, I will kill you." Whatever she injected him with didn't kill him but he was at a loss for words and couldn't move.

"If you call, text, email, jump your ugly ass on top of her or even go to family functions when she's there, I promise to have your entire family murdered." His eyes got really big.

"Ok gentlemen. Take this piece of shit outta here. I don't care where you drop him at." They lifted him up and that's the last time I saw or heard from him.

"Come down here Julie." I made my way to her. She put both hands on the side of my face.

"I love you as if I birthed you, and I'll protect you the same as I would Luna." I nodded.

"But if you come for any of us again, I will kill you." I stared at her.

"Don't look at me like that." She let go and went to grab her things.

"Oh. Make sure my grandkids come see me from time to time."

"But how, if daddy doesn't want me around?"

"Figure if out. Have a good night." And just like that, she was gone in the wind. Surprisingly, she and I met up a lot over the last two years. My kids loved her and the more we were around one another, my love for her grew. It was sad that I harbored so much hate for her in my younger years and our relationship had to be hidden. Hopefully, it'll change in the future.

"My kids are not yours." I shouted when I brought myself back from daydreaming.

"I think we should tell my son to get a DNA test and go from there."

"You know what? I think my stepmom would love to know you're threatening me again. What you think?" I heard a noise and looked down at my phone to see he hung up. *Punk ass.* Always talking shit about how big and bad he is and scarier than a two-year-old on Halloween.

****

"Where you going?" Oscar asked when he came in the room. We were still in Jersey waiting on him to catch Waleed.

"Taking the kids to the park." He gave me a weird look. I really am taking them but my stepmom is coming too. She hasn't seen them in a few days and claims to have clothes and other stuff. She spoils the hell outta them. I haven't told him yet because he'll assume it's a trap and try to keep me in.

"Oh ok. I'm coming." I looked up from tying my sneaker.

"Ugh, you don't have to. I know you're busy." He had me stand and wrapped his arms around my waist.

"It's fine. We haven't spent a lotta time together lately and I miss you."

"You're not worried someone will see you?"

"Babe, we have security just like everyone else. It'll be fine." I really did love this man.

Despite the beating he gave me for sleeping with Waleed, he's a good man and father. I'm not excusing him by no means for laying hands on me but I understand. Me tryna hurt Luna, hurt him and it was uncalled for. As far as I knew, he wasn't sleeping with anyone so it's like I cheated first.

"Ok then." We went to grab the kids, jumped in the truck and headed over. On the way my daughter asked a bunch of questions about toys, cartoons and other kid stuff, while my son took in the scenery from his window.

When the truck stopped my heart began to race. Oscar was taking the kids out and from the corner of my eye, my stepmother was pulling in. I could already picture the chaos about to erupt and prepared myself for it. I stepped out and before anyone could stop her, my daughter ran straight to her car.

"NANA! NANA!" Oscar looked at me as he held my son and I put my head down. However, nothing surprised me more than the other person getting out the passenger side. It's about to be a problem.

Luna

"Ma, why are we here?" I asked when she pulled up to some park. I was with her today running errands and shopping, as usual.

Waleed made me go sit in that movie theatre for two and a half hours the other day and I hated it. Then he had the nerve to cross his arms and say he was the Killmonger character. It was Wakanda this, Wakanda that. I wanted to kick his Wakanda ass and send him there. He had the nerve to say he was going to see it again because Raina wanted to go. I told him, peace. You won't have me sitting there again.

"I have to meet someone. You can stay in the car or get out. It's up to you." I stared at her because if she's giving me a choice as to stay in the car, something ain't right.

"Really?"

"What? It's clear you and this person can't stand each other. I'm only here for the little ones so don't start no shit." She cut the car off, popped the trunk and opened the door. I opened mine to see what she was getting, when a little girl came running over yelling out nana.

"Nana?" I questioned and my mom shrugged her shoulders. I'm her only child so who the hell kid is this calling her what my son will be doing soon?

"Whose kid is this and why is she calling you nana?" My mom ignored the question, lifted the kid up and placed a bunch of kisses on her face.

"Ma."

"What Luna." She kept kissing her.

"Her mother is over there." She pointed to Julie and all I wanted to do is bash her head into the ground. Oscar stood there with a little boy in his hand, appearing to be as lost as me.

"Are you fucking kidding me?" I turned to look at my mother who shrugged her shoulders. I started walking towards Julie and the bitch had the nerve to grab Oscar's hand.

"You are not my mothers' child. Why does that kid call her nana?"

"LUNA!" I heard my mom shout.

"Get over here right now." I stood there until I felt someone tugging at my pants. I looked down at the little girl and she favored my son. I thought about telling her to get off me, however I can't be mean to a child, even if I can't stand the mother.

"That's my mommy and daddy."

"I know. Can you go back over there?" My mom came over, gave Julie a hug and took her son from Oscar; well after he reached out for her. How long have they been in contact? It had to be a while if these kids know her.

"Let's sit down." My mom walked ahead of us and looked back with a stare telling us to come on.

The little girl, who I found out name is Maria, ran to the playground. My mom sat, while the three of us stood on the opposite side of her. The moment was awkward and you could feel the tension. I noticed Oscar nod his head no to some of his bodyguards as well. I wasn't worried because my father made my mom have her own and me as well. After Oscar's people shot the other ones, my father hired some damn assassins for us. So I'm sure they had guns drawn on Oscar's people now.

"Luna, I had no idea Oscar would be here or that you'd wanna tag along with me. Since you did, your sister and I have been in contact with one another for quite some time now."

"WHATTTTT? Does my father know? No, he can't because he would never be ok with this." I started pacing and Oscar began questioning Julie.

"No he doesn't and it's not up to you to inform him." She cradled the little boy in her arms.

"Ma. You can't really be ok with being in her life. She hated and tried to kill you. Had I not walked in, she would've." I was so mad, I sent a text to my husband and asked him to come here. Fuck that! He wanted Oscar so I'm handing him over.

"Luna, I understand your anger and frustration but I forgave her." I sucked my teeth.

"I'm not saying you have to but what you're not going to do is cause a scene out here in front of these kids. Nor are you going to mention this to your father."

"Ma."

"Maybe I didn't make myself clear." She stood and moved closer.

"When I'm ready and only then, I will tell him. Until then, you can continue being mad and keep any ill feelings to yourself." Just as she said that Waleed's truck pulled up and so did a bunch of other SUV's. They all jumped out with guns drawn and my mother was pissed. I stood there with my arms folded and shrugged my shoulders. At the end of the day, he's my husband and I can tell him what I want.

"What's this about?" Waleed asked walking up. Risky was next to him, while the others waited at their vehicles. You saw Oscar's people and ours. People in the park began running and some nosy motherfuckers stayed to watch. I never understood why people run to danger, instead of away from it.

"Evidently, my mom has been entertaining your ex and my father's child." He took a puff of his blunt, and looked at me, then Oscar.

"Oscar, I'm ready to get this shit over with. You ready to die?" He placed his gun at Oscar's temple and before I knew it, bullets were flying, my mother was screaming, Julie ran to grab her daughter and my ass was standing there stuck. I felt my body being pulled to the ground and looked to see one of my guards tryna get me outta here.

CLICK! I looked up and some guy had a gun to me and my bodyguards head. Literally two seconds later, his head exploded in front of me. Blood was on my face and clothes. I wiped some off and stared into the eyes of Julie who had the gun in her hand.

"LET'S GO!" Waleed snatched me up and had me ducking all the way to his truck.

"WAIT! Where's my mom?"

"She's fine." Once we got in, he went off on my ass.

"Why the fuck didn't you tell me there were kids out here?"

"Ugh, this is a park and my mom had the baby in her arms." He slammed on the brakes and stared at me.

"I wasn't paying attention and its damn near seven at night, so excuse me for assuming most kids are in the house. Let alone, I never got the time to survey my surroundings because you made it seem as if this Oscar nigga was at your neck."

"Waleed."

"Don't fucking Waleed me. You deliberately had me come for this nigga and he had kids out here. What if he did the same shit to you with my son? Who's to say he won't." I sat there listening to him rip me a new asshole.

"Then, you start talking that bullshit about Julie being my ex. Who the fuck cares? I married you. I gave you my son and most likely another kid."

"Waleed, you gave her one too." He chuckled and pulled off. When we got to our house he stepped out, came to my side, opened the door and made me get out. He closed the door, waited for the gate to open and went to get back in the truck.

"Where are you going?"

"To the fucking hospital. Because you were being so fucking petty, my brother got hit and so did Julie's son. Tha fuck is wrong with you." He sped out the driveway so fast, the tire marks were on the pavement. As bad as I wanted to go up to the hospital, I took my ass inside and just as I was about to get in the shower my doorbell rang. I opened it and my mother was on the other side. The look on her face showed anger and sadness.

"You know, I didn't think you'd be happy hearing about me forgiving Julie because she almost killed me and I get it." She pushed past me and stood in my living room.

"But for you to contact your husband and make him believe you were in danger knowing those kids were out there, is beyond reckless."

"Ma, I didn't know." She put her hand up.

"You knew good and damn well that man would come running, so save the lie for someone who wants to hear it. Then, you almost get killed and guess who saved your life?" I sucked my teeth. She gripped my chin forcefully and made me look at her.

"The two of you may have been at odds growing up but she didn't even think twice about pulling the trigger and you know why?" I remained silent.

"Because she grew up and matured, where you're still harboring hate for someone who didn't physically touch you. At that moment, regardless of your past, you were here sister, her kids' aunt and the only person who she couldn't dare allow die in front of her." I swung my face so she could no longer have it in her grip.

"How dare you come in my house and chastised me about my father's bastard child? Huh?" I started to walk away and stopped.

"You forget the day I walked in, and she was stabbing you to death. My own mother, who took care and raised this bitch as her own was being damn near murdered in front of me. You damn right, I can't stand her and beat her ass any chance I got. Ma, you were in the hospital for months, dad almost drank himself to death because of it and you're telling me she matured and its why she saved me."

"First off, don't ever in your fucking life disrespect me. I'll beat your ass like a bitch off the street and still come over the next day." I rolled my eyes when she wasn't looking. My mom is no joke with her hands.

"Second… let's not forget the torture you put her through growing up. You hated Julie for what your father did and always told her. There were times she'd cry her eyes out trying to figure out why you hated her? Why you bullied her in school and at the house? Why you told people she was your cousin and not your sister? How about the time you went to a party and left her there? She got drunk and was almost gang raped all because you were angry she was the life of the party and you weren't. Let's not forget how you beat her so bad, she ended up in ICU for a very long time too." I couldn't say a word because everything she spoke was true.

I hated Julie with every ounce of my body. I felt like her presence ruined my parents' marriage and if she weren't here, I wouldn't have missed those two years of being in a two-parent household. I blamed her mother for all the wrongdoings of my father and being she was dead, Julie felt the brunt of it. Call me childish but at the time, I was a child. Did I bully her? Absolutely! It's the exact reason I felt more than horrible for Raina who went through the same thing. The effects of someone humiliating, degrading, belittling and embarrassing you can mentally last a lifetime. I never told Raina because I didn't want her thinking differently of me.

"Ma, I can't forgive her for almost killing you or destroying our family."

"Then I feel sorry for you because the hate is only gonna consume you. Its gonna have you doing and saying dumb shit. I hope you don't lose your husband in the process." And with those last few words, she left me standing there.

Oscar

"How the fuck did this happen?" I paced back and forth in the hospital waiting room.

"Oscar, I…" Julie was about to speak when my father came strolling in. Where the hell did he come from and since when did he come to the states? He hated coming over here and vowed not to step foot in this place until the empire was mine.

"What are you doing here?" He looked at Julie, who had an evil look on her face. Now I was confused because I've never heard of them beefing.

"I heard my son was shot."

"Your son?"

"Yes, my son."

"Pops, I'm standing right here and as you can see, I'm fine. Now unless you have another child I don't know about, there's no kid of yours shot. Your grandson was hit in the leg and we're waiting for the doctors to come out." I told him and something about the way he stared at Julie didn't sit right with me.

"Should I tell him Julie, or do you want to?" All of a sudden, tears began to fall down her face.

"Oscar." Julie stood and kept my daughter on her hip.

"Well isn't this special?" Waleed said, stopping Julie from speaking.

"What the fuck you want?" I said and we stood toe to toe.

"Nothing right now because my boy is here but best believe when they say he's better, we'll speak." He shoulder checked me and started to walk away.

"So you're gonna just let him walk away?" My pops asked and I sat down.

"Like he said, now is not the time. My son is in surgery and so is his friend. Don't worry pops, I'll make sure to get things popping for you." He nodded and stood in front of Julie.

"Yo! Why you keep staring at her?"

"Fine! You don't wanna tell him Julie? I guess, I will."

"You'll do no such a thing." My mom came in and had the most hateful look on her face. What the hell is going on?

"Ma, what are you doing here?" She took Maria from Julie and sat down next to her.

"I received a call from an old friend that my grandchild was shot and took the jet here. Have we heard anything?"

"An old friend?"

"That's right. An old friend." I turned and it was Luna's mother.

"Ok, I'm lost. Can someone explain what's going on here?" Luna's mom and my mother led me in a room that was reserved for doctors to speak with family members who passed away. They called Julie in and the tears running down her face only made me wonder what was really going on. Luna's mom closed the door, sat next to Julie and waited for my mom to speak.

"Sit down son." I listened to my mom.

"Honey, what I'm about to tell you will come as a shock but trust me when I say, I had no idea. If I had, he

195

would've been dead already." I sat there watching Julie cry. Whatever it is must be really bad if she's still crying.

"A few years back when you were attending those business meetings for weeks at a time, you had your father checking on Julie, correct?"

"Yea."

"Ok. At first, he did what you asked." I nodded.

"One night, he arrived to your house drunk and Julie let him in. She left him on the couch and called me to say he was there. After hanging up, she went to bed and unfortunately; her and your dad had sex."

"SAY WHAT?" I jumped up off the couch and yoked Julie up right outta the chair.

CLICK! I looked and it was her father with a gun to my head.

"Put her down." It took me a few seconds to drop her but when I did, I spit on her.

"Oscar, please listen."

"You don't have shit to say to me. You're a fucking whore and I'm taking my kids. Hold up." I caught myself and turned to look at her again.

"Are those my kids?"

"Maria is but I'm not sure about lil Oscar." It was like my world came crushing down when she said that.

"You have a kid by me and my father? What type of shit is that?"

"If you sit yo ass down and listen, you'll understand." Luna's dad said. I was shocked he was even here. Last I heard, he wanted both of us dead.

"Son, he went in your bedroom and raped her."

"Nah. My dad don't need to rape anyone. She probably gave it up willingly." I could see the hurt on Julie's face.

"I know its hard to hear and I didn't believe it at first either."

"Then why do you believe it now?"

"Oscar, your father keeps a journal in the house he thinks I know nothing about. Actually, he writes in it daily. Needless to say, he wrote everything down. I'm assuming its something he used to do in jail and continued when he came home." My mom handed me two composition notebooks.

"Anyway, the first night he wrote how Julie was asleep and he wandered in her room and under the covers. The idiot even mentioned her calling your name." You could hear Julie crying hysterical.

"How long was it going on?"

"It happened a lot and he has threatened to kill Maria on plenty of occasions if she didn't comply. Sadly, she became pregnant and even though she was unsure of you fathering the child, she kept the secret to herself. The only reason he's attempting to hurt the kids now, is because you don't want to get this stupid empire and give it to him. Honey, your father has gone mad over it. He wants nothing more than to hurt Carlos for not including him after he left the jail." I heard my mother but my focus remained on Julie who couldn't stop crying.

"I need a minute with her."

"Don't put your hands on her." Her father said and they exited the room. At first, I didn't know what to say.

"I'm sorry for putting my hands on you and spitting. To think you slept with my father willingly did something to me."

"Oscar, I can't continue to be with you if you're going to beat on me. We have a daughter and I don't want her growing up thinking its normal and what about our son. He won't be a woman beater."

"I'm sorry and promise not to put hands on you again." I kissed her forehead as she laid her head on my shoulder.

"Why didn't you tell me?" She looked up at me.

"Look how you handled it when your mom told you. Had she not brought the diary and filled you in on his actions, I honestly don't see you believing me. Oscar, you had your father on a pedal stool. He could do no wrong in your eyes." I didn't say a word because she was right. I loved my father with everything in me. I may not have agreed with some of the things he taught and told me but he was still my pops.

"I can't believe he was doing that to you. Fuck! I'm so sorry you had to go through that. I blame myself for not watching over you better."

"You did everything right Oscar."

"I had cameras in the house. How did he get around them?"

"He knew exactly where they were and figured out a way to bypass them. He also knew there were none in the bedroom." She was right. I told my pops a few times, I didn't feel the need to have any in there because if anyone was in the house, I'd see them come in. Had I put some in there, I would've caught on sooner.

"I'm gonna kill him."

"Oscar?"

"I have to Julie, otherwise; he'll try and take my son and I can't have that." She looked at me.

"That's my motherfucking son. I don't care what he says."

"Do you wanna get a test?" She asked.

"Hell no!"

"Oscar, we should know."

"Julie, I don't want to. I was there when he was born. I've been raising him since birth. No test is gonna tell me he's not mine."

"Oscar, where do we go from here? He's gonna try and take him. Oh my God, where is he?" She said and we both jumped up and ran out.

"Where is he?" I asked my mom and Waleed answered.

"Oh that no good nigga father of yours left and told me to give you a message." We both looked at him.

"He said, he's coming for his son and no one can stop him." I felt Julie squeeze my hand.

"Oscar." I know she was telling me to get the test so we can know for sure.

"Fine. Set it up. I'll have the results fixed if he's not mine." She nodded and went to the nurses' station. I pray to God that he's mine.

****

"You are 99.999999% the father." Is what Julie said when she read the results of the paternity test we took yesterday.

After my father left and Waleed gave me the message, I made the nurses take a test ASAP. Hell yea, I planned on changing the results if I weren't the father, who wouldn't?

Luckily, he was indeed mine and I made sure to send a screen shot picture to my father's phone. Julie was happy as hell and to be honest, I was too. I would've still loved my son but it probably would have been weird to know he was my brother and I'd raise him as my son.

"Daddy." My daughter came running in the room smiling. We took a test for her as well, just so my father didn't try and say she was his either. There was no doubt in my mind about my daughter and after finding out the horrible things he did to my girl, at least we know for sure.

"Hey lil mama. Who brought you here?"

"I did." My mom said and had a disturbing look on her face.

"What's wrong?" Julie asked and picked my son up. He just woke up from the surgery last night and I had to make her leave him in the crib so his body could rest. She was a nervous wreck from mentioning the things with my father, to our son being shot. I held her in my arms on that tight ass hospital couch all night.

"Your father put a hit out on both of you."

"For what?"

"Evidently, you're not loyal and Julie is spreading lies."

"Oscar, we need to leave. Between him and Waleed wanting us dead, we have to go."

"She's right son. Let's not take the chance of someone killing y'all." She lifted my son outta Julie's arms.

"I'm not running." I picked my phone up.

"Oscar."

"Let me make some calls." I stepped out the room and set up a meeting with someone I dreaded to ever come in contact with.

Khloe

"How you feeling baby?" I asked Ryan who was shot in the side yesterday. I'm not even sure of everything that went down. Waleed only called and said I had to get to the hospital. When I went, my ass was a nervous wreck and never bothered to ask how it happened.

"I'm ok. How are you?" He tried to sit up. You could see the pain he was in as he pressed the button for the bed to lift.

"Now that you're ok, I'm fine. Do you want me to get the nurse?"

"No. Where's Raina?"

"Downstairs getting food with my mother in law." I rolled my eyes.

"Why you do that?"

"Between her and Raina, they are driving me crazy about this baby."

"What you mean?"

"Ryan, do you know they went crib and stroller shopping already? My daughter posted the damn 3D ultrasound picture on her Instagram. And your mom told everyone and I've been receiving phone calls about a baby shower and a bunch of other stuff." He busted out laughing.

"Ryan, don't laugh."

"I'm trying not to but it's funny." I folded my arms.

"Come here baby." He reached his arm out and slid over slowly so I could sit with him.

"They love you just as much as I do and we're all happy you're pregnant. Shit, I'm ready to put another one in you already." I wanted to smack him on the arm but stopped myself.

"K, Raina just turned thirteen, which means there hasn't been a baby around in years." I looked at him because Luna and the baby were at the house all the time.

"Lil Wale is at the house a lot but he's not ours."

"I guess you're right."

"You guess huh." He rubbed my belly.

205

"Not too much longer. I can't wait to meet you." He loved talking to the baby in my stomach. I pressed the nurses button for them to let the doctor know he was awake. He wanted to get cleaned up and sit in the chair. Talking about old people stay in bed all day.

Once I finished helping him wash, his mom and Raina were walking in the room. They brought me some food and all of us stayed up here all day. Waleed came but when I asked where Luna was, he claimed not to know. I called and text her all day and she only responded to the first message, saying she wasn't feeling well and would speak to me later. Whatever they had going on must've pissed him off bad because he claimed he was staying at our house.

"Ryan, can we talk?" I asked when everyone left. Of course, I'm staying the night.

"What's up babe?" He was watching some basketball game.

"Am I fat to you?" He snapped his neck.

"Hell no."

"But I gained some weight from the baby and what if I get bigger? Are you gonna leave me? What if I can't drop the weight after the baby?" He took his hand and made me face him.

"Stop worrying about the small things."

"I'm scared Ryan. I was already kinda big when we got together, I've gained ten pounds with the baby and.-" I just started crying.

"And you look beautiful. Khloe, you have my son or daughter in you so it's expected for you to gain weight. So what if you can't drop it afterwards, it won't stop me from loving you. And if you wanted to work it off at the gym, I'd go with you."

"Do you want me to lose weight? Is that why you said something about the gym?"

"Nope. If you don't wanna go, don't. If you want to and need a partner, I'll go. I want you to do whatever you want, as long as that pussy gets super wet and have me moaning, I could care less." I laughed at his silliness.

"Are you ashamed of me?"

"No." I looked at him.

"In the beginning, I admit it was hard to be seen with you. But now, any and everyone knows we're together. They know you're having my baby, marrying me and adopting my daughter." I smiled thinking about how him and Raina asked me the other day to legally adopt her. She had balloons and everything. It was cute and I cried when they showed me the papers.

"I just don't want you to get bored or say I'm getting too big."

"Never. Now take yo ass to sleep. You're interrupting my game." He put the covers over me and laid back. I felt him move my head on his chest and his arm was wrapped around me. I need to stop thinking bad thoughts and enjoy him loving me, otherwise I'm gonna drive myself crazy.

****

"Are you coming to the baby shower ma?" Ryan's mom was throwing it and wanted a head count. I may not care for my mother but I won't leave her out. Ryan was out the hospital for two weeks now and home resting so he too was helping set it up.

If you wondering why I'm with her its because took her to the doctors. My father was working and couldn't. She was still having headaches from what Veronica did to her. And Ryan didn't make it any better by dragging her by the hair when he thought she sliced my face up.

"Not if your baby daddy or that immigrant is gonna be there." I stopped and looked at her.

"Ma, I'm over this attitude and your hateful ways." We were standing outside the office now.

"Excuse me."

"Ma, I have endured the hatred, bullying and embarrassment all my life and I'm done. You have done nothing except kick me when I'm down and now that my fiancé has shown me what true love is, I refuse to allow you to continue."

"True love, huh?" She threw her head back laughing.

"That punk ass nigga is just like the rest of these men out here. You think because he knocked your fat ass up and put a ring on it, he's gonna be faithful? Think again honey. He may have locked you down but the fact remains you're still fat and it's all you'll ever be." The more she spoke, the angrier I became.

"Well at least he's not gonna be jealous of his own son if we have one. He won't call him names and disrespect him in public."

"Girl please. I'm not the only one who called you those names and no need to be jealous when you were bigger than me. Why would I be jealous of that? Ain't like I wanted to be your size." She tried to open my car door but I kept it locked and walked over to her.

"Don't walk up on me. Fuck around and get your ass beat."

"You would fight a pregnant woman? Your own daughter at that."

"Hell yea. Shit you old enough to hit me or talk tough then expect to get it back. Now get your fat ass in..." I cut her off when my first connected to the side of her face.

"Oh you wanna fight bitch?" She dropped her purse and actually tried to swing. I hit her again and again until someone lifted me off.

"GET OFF ME!" I yelled at the person and turned around to see Marcus standing there with a cane. I could hear the cops in the distance.

"Are you ok?"

"I'm fine." I fixed my clothes and went to get in my truck. I rolled the window down when he knocked on it.

"Khloe, I've been looking for you."

"For what?"

"To repay your boyfriend for crippling me." He pointed a gun at me.

"Marcus what are you doing?" He had the gun on my temple.

"I've had four knee surgeries and I can barely perform in the bedroom. Your man made sure I wouldn't walk without a cane again. He took away my confidence and it's only fair I take something from him."

"Marcus don't do this. I'm pregnant." I had my hand in my purse searching for the mace. It's not a gun but I'm sure it'll do the job and give me time to bounce.

"Too bad." His finger pulled back on the trigger at the same time I sprayed him. He started choking and my ass sped outta there. The cops were coming in at the same time. Hopefully, they saw him with the gun and arrest his ass.

I drove straight to the hospital and called Ryan. I needed to make sure my baby was ok. He's gonna have a fit and wanna kill my mother and it's sad to say, I don't have a problem with it.

Ryan

"I'll be there to get you after I drop Khloe off." I told Waleed on the way home from the hospital. I hung up and took her hand in mine. Not only was she nervous and upset about fighting her mother but that cornball ass motherfucker had the nerve to pull a gun on her.

After finding Khloe at the Hilton with his bum ass, I had Waleed go there and make sure he knew Khloe was off limits. I couldn't go because if I saw them, they'd both be dead and since Raina was with me, it was a good thing. That same night, I had my mom come over to sit with Raina while we went to the hospital to inform him of the no snitching rule. He had the nerve to start crying.

Waleed though it was funny where my gut told me not to trust him. I planned on killing him the moment he left the hospital but he said the nigga was harmless. Now look. He came back for me and found my fiancé, attempted to kill her and is probably gonna try again. Ain't no way in hell I'm allowing shit to slide. My side may still be in pain; however, my woman will never walk this earth in fear. And I have a trick for her mom.

"Ryan, I want you to stay in with me tonight." We both knew it was to keep me from getting them. Any other time I'd be with it but not tonight. I had eyes on both of those idiots.

"I'll be home before you close those pretty eyes of yours."

"Ryan."

"Khloe I'm gonna to be fine. I want you to go in the house, take a bath and relax. Throw on some Netflix and I promise to chill with your sexy ass when I'm done." She started laughing. I parked in front of the house and my mom opened the door. Yea, she's been over here a lot to help out with me, Raina, and Khloe who has been extremely tired with the pregnancy.

"Please be careful."

"Always baby." I went to her side of the car, pecked her lips and helped her out.

"Don't forget to give Raina some.-"

"You better not say Zzquil." She would get so mad when I offered some sleep remedy for Raina. I'd never give it to her but the reactions were always funny.

"Why not? There's no narcotics in that. It's just a sleep suppressant and you know I haven't felt inside of you since the shooting. Babe, I need to hear you screaming and moaning."

"I promise to make sure you hear me but she's not getting any sleep suppressant."

"Fine! Just make sure she sleep. Hell, her ass will be up later than us." I can come home at two in the morning, and Raina will be on the couch or in her room watching television and on her phone.

One day I asked her why and she said and I quote, *"daddy kids my age don't go to sleep early. We stay up half the night on Instagram and snap chat."* I have no idea what would possess them to keep refreshing and scrolling down some page just to double tap and hit like. It's crazy and yet, these kids love it.

"I'll see you in a few."

"Ok." We kissed, I locked the door and headed out.

****

"So you're telling me, Khloe's mom and ex came for her in one day?" Waleed asked as we waited inside Marcus house. We could've waited in the car but we were bored and decided to see how this nigga was living.

"I don't think either of them want her to be happy. Look at this shit." I showed him all the different medications on the dresser.

"Nigga probably addicted. What you think?"

"Most likely." I moved around the room and we heard a door shut. Waleed and I started walking down the steps. You could hear him speaking to someone on the phone and the closer we got, it was clear as day that the person was Khloe's mother. We stood there listening and spoke when he hung up.

"What type of funeral you want Marcus?" He jumped and turned around.

"Yo! You nasty as hell." Waleed pointed to the wet spot in the front of his pants.

"Wha... what... are you doing here?" I stood there with my arms folded.

"Well, my fiancé called me and said she got into a fight with her mom and as she was tryna leave, some man pulled a gun out on her. Do you happen to know who would've done such a thing? I mean who would be that stupid, knowing she's my woman?" I looked at Waleed who picked the remote up to the television and turned it on.

"I don't know." His body began to shake with fear.

"Its crazy right?" I smiled and moved closer.

"My woman is the sweetest person I know, yet; people continue to try her." I pushed him on the chair.

"Why did you have him shoot me in my legs?" He pointed to Waleed who was engrossed in the basketball game.

"Oh! That's an easy and fair question." I pulled the gun out my waist and screwed on the silencer. Usually, I'd handle murders in another place, however; I can see this idiot screaming bloody murder if we left this house. Plus, he has a ton of neighbors.

"I told you at the club not to answer her call because I'd kill you and your kids. Do you remember?" He swallowed hard.

"And what did you do?" His head went down.

217

"Then you had the audacity to fuck her knowing I'd be lurking."

"She said, you two were no longer together." I snickered at his dumb response.

"We weren't together the night at the club either but who did she go home with?"

"You." He whispered.

"Exactly! That should've told you to leave her alone so I'm gonna ask you again, how you want your funeral?"

"Why are you asking me that?"

"Oh, I guess K didn't tell you. I own a funeral home and everyone uses me. I'm sure your family will contact me to pick your body up." His eyes grew big.

"What color do you want to wear and would you prefer makeup or not?" My gun was on his forehead and tears were falling down his face.

"Please! I have kids."

"So do I and Khloe is pregnant, which you know because she screamed it out as you held the gun to her head." Waleed turned to look at me.

218

"Wait! Ask him about the mother." I lifted my finger off the trigger but kept my gun on him.

"Why were you on the phone with her?"

"She wants Khloe beat up really bad and asked me to pay some chicks off the street to do it."

"WHAT?" I was fuming.

"She hates Khloe and always has. When we were in a relationship she tried to sleep with me on a few occasions, when I didn't she threatened to tell Khloe about my kids."

"Hold up! Her mom knew you were cheating on her?" He nodded his head yes.

"She caught me out with the woman a few times. Her mom is the one who had my kids mother show up at Khloe's graduation at the same time I proposed."

"She grimy as fuck." Waleed shouted.

"She is and if you don't get her, Khloe is only going to continue dealing with it."

"Thanks bro, but I got this."

PHEW! PHEW! Waleed looked at me and I shook my head. Khloe has dealt with a lotta shit in the past and this is only going to hurt her worse.

"Are you gonna tell her?"

"I don't even know. What you think?"

"We need to find out who he hired to fight her, if he did at all and worry about the mother ASAP." I agreed and once the clean-up was done, we all ransacked the apartment to make it look like a robbery gone wrong. I could've dumped the body but why would I do that, when I can get paid to bury him? Shit, money is money, no matter how you get it.

On the ride over to see Khloe's mom, all I could think about is the fact she hated her daughter and wanted to hurt her. I've heard of jealous parents but she is ridiculous with it. I made a phone call on the way for someone to meet us. Unfortunately, after my fiancé hears what her mother has been up to, I'm sure its gonna hurt her even more. Maybe, I won't tell her until after the baby is born. I can't have her stressing herself out over nonsense because that's all it is.

We pulled up at Khloe's mom at the same time her dad did. He stepped out and thanked me for allowing him to come witness this. I'm not sure if killing her is the answer, but I'm for sure gonna instill enough fear in her so she knows if anything happens to Khloe, that'll be the end of her existence.

"Oh shit. You got a key?" Waleed asked and her dad turned to look with a grin on his face.

"What are you doing here and why are they with you?" She snapped the minute he opened the door. I guess she was getting ice for her eye because he didn't even have to call her downstairs.

"Let's talk." I grabbed her by the arm and she tried to fight me off.

"Get your fucking hands off me. Wait, til I tell Khloe." All of us stared at her like she was crazy. Did this hateful bitch really say that? I tossed her on the couch and Khloe's dad had a hateful look on his face.

"What?" She questioned.

"Why did you put hands on Khloe?" Her dad asked.

"Are you serious? She swung on me first and.-"

"And she's pregnant. Had you not antagonized her, maybe she wouldn't have."

"Antagonized her? She started talking shit to me and I wasn't about to let her disrespect me. If she gave a fuck about that bastard baby, she wouldn't have opened her mouth." I jumped off the couch and Waleed stood in front of me.

"You see the type of man you're allowing your daughter to have a baby with and marry? He's ignorant, dangerous and probably has a bunch of kids all over." She rolled her eyes.

"What the fuck is wrong with you? Do you really hate your daughter that much?" I asked and outraged by her answer.

"I don't give a fuck about that fat bitch. She's the reason I couldn't have any more kids and my brothers don't speak to me."

"You know that's not true." Her father said.

"Yes, it is. She was so fat coming out she ruptured my insides. Then, my brothers catered to her more than me and even went to war with me over it. She ruined my life so hell yea, I spent all of my time, ruining hers and don't plan on stopping." We all looked at her.

"Oh you think I don't have plans for her?" She threw her head back laughing.

"Well, if you're depending on Marcus to carry them out, I hate to be the one to tell you this but he's not gonna be able to do anything where he's at." I gave her a fake smile and her eyes got big. Now it was my turn to dig in her ass.

"See, in the beginning I was ashamed of my girl and it took a lot of soul searching within myself to realize my own insecurities came from hateful and envious people like you."

"Excuse me."

"Yea, its individuals in this world who would rather tear people down, due to their appearance instead of building them up."

"Whatever." She waved her hand.

"I used to say the same thing to my mother when she said those same words to me. However, Khloe entered my life and everything I thought I knew about wanting a bad bitch went out the window. You see, Khloe may not be a model to the outside world but she is to me. That woman can make me do a double and triple take when she walks in a room. Her confidence, appearance and personality are what makes her the woman she is and I'm glad she didn't feel sorry for herself all these years and became a better person."

"Please. She's weak."

"That's where you're wrong. Khloe, is one of the strongest women I know. She held my daughter down before knowing I was her father. She went to war for her and believe it or not, left me when she felt I didn't respect her. It took a lot of begging to get her back and I thank God everyday she found it in her heart to forgive me but you. You're hell bent on making her suffer for things she had absolutely no control over." She didn't say anything.

"All Khloe wanted was for her mother to love her, the way she loved you. Unfortunately, you were stuck on jealousy and started making her buy you things with her hard earn money. In her eyes, she thought it was the right thing to do when in fact, all it did was cause more harm than good. But let me fill you in on a secret." I stood in front of her.

"That woman is going to be my wife, the mother of my kids and in no way, shape or form are you going to continue harassing her." I pulled my gun out and lifted her chin with the tip of it to look at me. I witnessed the tears falling down her face and gave no fucks.

"You have a choice to make and hopefully you choose right because your decision will be your fate of living or dying." Her father came and stood next to me. I could tell he was upset as well but he didn't say a word.

"From this day forward, you are not allowed to contact my future wife, nor will you see my kids. No birthdays, holidays, christenings, nothing. If by some chance she contacts you, I won't say anything unless she tells me you disrespected her." I let my finger sit on the trigger and her breathing increased.

"If I leave this house and you mention this to her or the cops, I won't hesitate to return and do you the same as Marcus. Do I make myself clear?" She nodded her head yes. I backed up, put the gun away and stared at Khloe's dad shaking his head at her. I went to leave and turned around.

"Oh, Mrs. Banks make sure if you do decide to be slick and say something, you have your colors picked out for the funeral, I'll be sure to perform the services at." Her mouth hung open.

"Waleed, you think she'll need makeup?"

"Nah, she needs to go to hell looking just like that." He hit her with the peace sign and I nodded. Now that, that's over, its time to deal with Oscar and his father.

Waleed

I stepped in my crib for the first time in days since the shit with Luna at the park. I missed the hell outta her but she needed to learn that what she did was reckless as fuck. Not only did my boy get hurt but a baby as well. Thank goodness it was only a flesh wound on the child because Luna's mom shielded him but still. An injury on a kid is still painful and Luna should know that. Hell, she be ready to fight when the doctor gives my son an immunization shot.

I smelled food cooking and walked in the kitchen to see her playing with my son in the bouncy chair. I leaned on the wall and stared at my family. I can't imagine what Oscar went through when his son was hit, and I don't want to. Say what you want but beefing or not, I'd never wish harm on a child. After a few minutes of watching, I went upstairs and hopped in the shower. Not too long after my wife stepped in and had tears in her eyes. Instead of asking what was wrong, I kissed her and the two of us started feeling each other up.

"I missed you baby." She moaned out when I entered her. There was no foreplay or anything. This right here was straight fucking and she knew it.

"Don't ever pull no bullshit like that again. I don't care how mad you are. Do you understand?" She nodded and bit down on my shoulder as I brought her to the first orgasm.

"Waleed, I'm pregnant." I stopped and let her down.

"How do you know already? It hasn't been long since we had sex without me pulling out."

"There's a test you can take a few days after sex and it tells you." They really make anything these days.

"Well, then I won't be pulling out." I turned her around and bent her over.

"Did you turn the food off?"

"Yes."

"Where's my son?"

"Asleep in the swing. Oh fuck!" She grabbed on the side of my legs.

"Good, we have a good hour at least to let me finish getting these frustrations out." I fucked the hell outta my wife and passed out on the bed. Her pussy had a way of making me do that. She ended up going to get my soon and put him the bed with us. He still got up a short time later but at least we weren't worried about him being alone downstairs.

****

"What now Dora?" I saw her standing outside some building when I came out the store. I was picking some things up for Luna. She wanted to try some freaky shit Khloe told her about and I was all for it. She asked for some whip cream, strawberries, handcuffs and a few other things and why wouldn't I get it? She wasn't gonna be with another nigga so any tricks she had up her sleeve were strictly for me anyway.

"I wanted to know if you knew where your wife was?"

"Dora, why are you obsessing over my wife?"

"I'm just saying. You act like she perfect and I know for a fact she's in this building with a bunch of men."

"Yea right."

"Oh no. Watch this." She knocked on the door and some guy opened it. We went in and it appeared to be some sort of restaurant but my wife wasn't in here." She appeared to be stuck on stupid too. I went to leave when a door opened and smoke came out behind him.

"Waleed. My nigga, what's up?" Some guy I knew from around the way asked.

"Not much. What's good with you?"

"Shit. You here to get your wife?" When he said that Dora smirked.

"Yea. How long she been here?" I asked trying to hide my anger. I don't know if I were angrier at her being here or Dora's dumb ass thinking she was cheating.

"Over the last few days; all the time. She made a lotta money down there." My antennas went up and I hurried him to take me to her. He walked to the door he came out of and if you weren't looking, you wouldn't even know it was there. I figured it was some illegal shit going on and they didn't want anyone to know about it.

He opened it, we made our way down some spiral steps and there was a huge room filled with men and women. I didn't see my wife anywhere but the other women in there seemed to be tryna figure out who I was. I knew quite a bit of the men in here and spoke to them in passing. After following dude a few more feet, he stopped at a table and the first person who saw me is Khloe.

"My boy know you here?" Luna jumped at the sound of my voice and Khloe sucked her teeth.

"Waleed what are you doing here and how did you? Hmph, I should've known your bloodhound was with you." She rolled her eyes and continued playing the game of poker.

"Bloodhound, says the woman who's down here with a bunch of men, doing God knows what." It never did take my wife long to jump on her. As she beat the shit outta Dora, I picked her cards up and continued playing for her. I don't know how but my wife had a win in her hands.

"How much is that for my wife?" One of the guys sucked his teeth.

"100 k. I'm not playing with her anymore. Man, your wife whoops our ass in this game every time." I smiled at her as she wiped the dirt off her jeans.

"That means she's doing well for herself." I yanked her by the hair and threw my tongue in her mouth.

"Don't put your hands on another bitch while you're pregnant with my baby. Do I make myself clear?" She nodded and grabbed her things to leave.

"You pregnant again." Mr. S, came outta a different room with Oscar and Julie. "Daddy, what the hell is going on?" I guess we were on the same page with this.

"Let's go Khloe." She stood and grabbed her things as well.

"Waleed, I'm not ready to go. I want my father to tell me.-" I cut her off.

"Never discuss family business in front of motherfuckers you don't know. If its that important step outside." She pouted but did like I asked. Once we got out there, I saw someone dragging Dora out the door.

"Do me a favor and take her to the spot. I'm tired of her causing problems in my daughters' marriage." It was then I knew Dora would never grace my presence again and I was happy.

"Its time Waleed."

"Time for what?" She questioned and her father looked at me and she stared at Julie and Oscar. I sent a message to Risky and told him the same thing her father told me. He already knew where the meeting spot was and said he was on the way.

"Go straight to Khloe's."

"Huh?" I grabbed her hand and walked away from everyone.

"Don't ask questions and do what I said."

"Are you gonna be ok?"

"Yes. Now go and don't make any stops. I don't care if you have to pee. Hold it until you get there. My mom is there with the baby."

"Ok. Be careful with whatever you're about to do."

"Always. Text me when you get there and even if I don't text you back, don't worry I will respond when I get a chance." She nodded and walked to Khloe's truck. I kissed her and watched them pull off.

"Let's get rid of this motherfucker." I said and hopped in one of the SUV's that pulled up.

Oscar

"Son, be careful. He has a whole team out there searching and ready to kill you." My mom said on the phone.

"I'm good ma. We're about to leave now." I told her and watched Julie strap the bulletproof vest around me. We were standing in the parking lot of Risky's funeral home getting ready to get my father.

"Where are my grandkids?"

"With Julie's mom." Ever since they began speaking again that's what my wife calls her. Yes, we were married, thanks to her father who had his friend do it on short notice.

"Good. I'll be there this weekend."

"Ok. See you then." I hung up and took Julie hands in mine.

"I'm gonna be fine baby." She nodded and wiped her eyes.

The day my mother came in the hospital to warn me about my father, I made the dreadful call to Julie's father. I didn't want to but if this was to end we had to come together and get my father. Unfortunately, he still had a few connections and people who were dying to work for him. They too were under the impression, he'd get the empire and employee each of them. My pops is an asshole and most likely had no intention of doing shit for them. He's greedy and the less people he had to pay, the better.

Anyway, Mr. S agreed to meet up with me and we had a heart to heart, with Julie present. They both said some shit to one another, she broke down and cried. His wife came in and she too cried and told Julie she understood and forgave her a long time ago. She also mentioned Luna would probably never get over it and she doesn't blame her. To watch a parent almost die is hard and she's never gotten over it.

During the meeting, Waleed and Risky showed up and he had us squash the beef. Of course, Waleed wasn't tryna hear it at first because of what happened at the mall but he smoked a few blunts and shit was good afterwards. I thought, I smoked a lot but he had me beat.

"Oscar please come back to me." She said and fell into my arms. I thought she was being dramatic until she didn't move.

"Julie? Julie?" I lifted her up and she had tears coming down her face.

"What's wrong?"

"Oh shit, she's bleeding." Someone yelled out and everyone turned around. Her father ran over. She had a bullet in her side and blood was pouring out.

"Who shot her?" When he said that, another guy dropped in front of us. We looked and there were men on top of the building across the street.

"FUCK! He's here. Get her inside." I lifted her up and begged her to stay awake.

"Oscar, its hurting."

"I know baby. I'm taking you to the hospital."

"Its ok. Make sure you take care of the kids." She said quietly and whoever jumped in the front seat, sped off in route to the hospital.

"Stay awake Julie."

"I can't."

"HURRY UP!" I shouted to the driver and felt the truck pick up speed. When we got there Julie was barely breathing. The doctors took her straight in the back. I called her mom and told her what happened. She got here in less than twenty minutes.

"Where are my kids?"

"With Luna." I stopped her from going to the nurses' station.

"I know its weird but there was no other option. Oscar, she won't let anything happen to them."

"Are you sure?"

"Positive. She may hate you two but she'd never take it out on kids." I tried to understand but I was still worried.

"Go find that bastard and make him regret ever being born." Me and the driver hopped back in the truck and made our way to where I knew my pops would be.

See, my father may not come here a lot but the few times he did, he always found her. If you're wondering who her is, its his mistress. They've been dealing with one another for years. He assumed no one knew about her but I did and its why we're pulling down the street in front of her house now.

I saw two guards pacing the front of her house, which only verified him being here. I put the window down a little, pointed my gun at them and watched their bodies hit the pavement. I made a call to Mr. Suarez and let him know where I was. He said, they just finished getting rid of all the people shooting at them and they were on the way. He tried to get me to wait but I couldn't. My wife was fighting for her life and its because of him.

I turned the doorknob and it was open just like she said it would be. Oh yea, his mistress wanted nothing to do with him. She told me if he ever came to town again, she'd tell me and if she couldn't and I found out, the door would always be unlocked. I guess she wasn't lying because here I am, with my gun pointed at my father who was coming out the bathroom butt ass naked. His mistress ran out the room.

"You found me huh?" He said and began putting his boxers on.

"Pussy has always been your downfall." He said and shook his head in disgust.

"Nah, pops. It was yours, which is why you raped my wife."

"Your wife." I smiled.

"Exactly! My wife."

"And here I thought she'd give me some more pussy." I let a shot off and hit him in the stomach. He yelled out and stared at me. I didn't wanna kill him just yet. He needed to feel some sort of pain before dying.

"I never in my life thought I'd be the one to take your life but after hearing what you did to my wife, its only right." His eyes got really big and I didn't know why until I turned around and saw a woman standing there.

"Have fun in hell." Luna said and shot him in between the eyes. I thought she was at the house with my kids.

"What are you doing here? Where are my kids?"

"He raped my sister multiple times and tried to kill her tonight. I know he's your father and you wanted to take his life but I needed to do it. And the kids are with Khloe."

"But why?"

"I tortured the fuck outta her when we were young. I blamed her for everything and it wasn't right. She isn't the reason my father was unfaithful and I made her feel like she was." She started crying and Waleed walked in.

"She forgave you a long time ago Luna." Julie wanted to hate her but after the shit with Waleed, she told me there was no need to hurt her anymore and she as well understood the hate Luna had towards her.

"I'm probably the reason she tried to kill my mom anyway so its only fair, I kill the man who tried to take everything from her."

"Julie is my wife and what she did is fucked up on all levels but don't blame yourself for her actions. She knew damn well what she was doing, which is why she takes full responsibility. Luna, you have every right to hate her regardless of the torture you put her through. However, she will be happy to know you killed him and forgive her."

"I doubt it."

"No she will. Its been weighing heavy on her too." She hugged me and went over to Waleed who was waiting for her.

"Bro, don't let my wife hug you again." Luna and I both started laughing.

"I'm serious, I don't want no old feelings to resurface."

"Waleed, be quiet. If I said that to you about Julie, you'd be ripping me a new asshole."

"I'm just saying." He said.

"You're not saying anything. Let's go with your annoying ass."

"Annoying. Oh hell no. Let's see how annoying we are when?-" He whispered something in her ear and she smacked him on the arm. Luna's mom did say they argued a lot and that their relationship was comical and I can see it for myself.

"You ok son." Mr. Suarez asked when he came in.

"Yea. At least, we don't have to worry about him anymore."

"Nope and I wanna talk to you about something." He walked out the door with me and sent the clean-up people inside. He said a few words to me and we headed over to the hospital. When we got there the doctor came out an hour later and filled us in on Julie's status and a nigga cried hearing the good news.

Epilogue

Khloe and Ryan, had a son they named after him. Raina

was adopted shortly after and she called her mommy every day.

Khloe also made sure, Raina went to see her mom at least once

a week and any other time she wanted. They tied the knot six

months after the baby was born and of course, Ryan knocked

her up again. Raina asked them to wait a few years before the

next one because there's no way she was babysitting three

small kids at once.

Khloe's mom tried to reach out and apologize but after

years of her bullying her, the verbal, and mental abuse nothing

she did would make Khloe speak to her. Her dad refused to

deal with her after finding out she fought K at the doctor's

office and now has a girlfriend. He still loved his ex-wife but

he had enough. Raina continued therapy but at a different

office and she was getting better than ever. She even

volunteered down at the woman's shelter and spoke to some of the teenagers who went through the same thing she did. Her grades were now excellent and she had all Advanced classes when she went to high school. She did drop a few pounds but said she liked being thick and no one would make her feel different.

Luna and Waleed are still quite the comical couple and are on their next baby too. They're getting remarried in a big wedding next year. Luna, wanted to make sure Khloe had her moment because she deserved it. After the shit Dora pulled at the card game and Luna beat her ass, she was never heard from again. Ashley, finally gave up the search for Veronica and went on with her boring and ghetto life.

Julie recovered from the gunshot and in the process, they found out she was expecting again, which is why Oscar was so happy. They ended up moving to the states and his mom came along. She said, he wasn't keeping her grandkids away. Julie went to thank Luna for avenging Oscar's father shooting her and the two of them literally had a crying fest. I don't know who cried more. It was so much snot and tears, the guys left their asses inside and smoked their lives away in the back.

Last but not least, Waleed and Oscar decided that since neither of them wanted the empire they'd give it back to Luna's father. However, he didn't want it and had them split up territory. They didn't have to do any work and reaped the benefits of the money flowing in.

Overall, everyone got what they wanted and who knew they'd all become close? I guess dealing with so much bullshit its only right to put it behind you and move on. The hate wasn't gonna get us anywhere. Forgiveness can be the key to a lifetime of happiness, in some cases.

The End

To all my readers,

I hope you enjoyed reading this series as much as I enjoyed writing it. I stepped out the box to hit on different issues and to know it was appreciated, makes it all worth it. Thank you all so much for the support and I'm gonna try and keep you entertained with my stories. Love you all.

Please remember that even though this book is fiction, there are people who are going through this every day. Just because you, someone you know, a family member and etc… aren't dealing with these type of issues, please don't assume its not happening. What you may go through, isn't always what someone else is. What you allow, isn't the same as what someone else will allow. Don't make assumptions when you don't know what's really going on.

If this book series has touched one person, then I did my job and I hope they become stronger and get through whatever it is, they may be going through. We are living in different times and everything isn't always what it seems.

If you or anyone you know has been bullied, or contemplating suicide please talk to someone. You can also contact the suicide hotline. Some may know it and others may not. I listed it down below in case someone needs them.

National Suicide Prevention Hotline

(There is also an online chat if you don't want to speak to someone directly)

1-800-273-8255

Cyber bully Hotline

1-800-420-1479

National Center For Missing and Exploited Children Cyber Tipline

1-800-843-5678

CPSIA information can be obtained
at www.ICGtesting.com
Printed in the USA
LVHW011658180119
604419LV00014B/571/P

9 781987 610147